Scary Short Stories
October 2023
Back Roads Literary Review

Michael Van Natta, Editor

ISBN: 979-8-9884904-2-5 (Paperback). Any references to historical events, real people, or real places are used fictitiously. Some of the places depicted are fictitious embellishments of actual places but beyond that, names, characters, and places are products of the author's imagination.

Printed by Ingram Spark, Inc., in the United States of America.

First printing edition 2023.

Back Roads Literary Review
1699 Highway 14
Knoxville, IA 50138

www.backroadsliteraryreview.com

Table of Contents

FOREWORD

Michael Van Natta
Editor in Chief

In the land of literature, there exists a dark and enigmatic dirt road, a place where words are spoken in whispers, where boundaries between reality and nightmares blur. This is a realm woven from the threads of ancient folklore, whispers in the night, and a primal fear that has echoed through the ages.

Welcome, dear readers, to this sinister anthology of short stories that beckon you to traverse a murky path, where the heartbeat quickens, where the fight or flight instinct threatens rationality.

Scary storytelling and writing are deep within our natures, whether as a means to understand the unknowable, or cautionary tales of choices and consequences Contemplating the nature of good and evil, we have always sought and struggled with a need to explore the unknown.

At the very dawn of the earliest civilizations, these tales served a dual purpose: to entertain and to caution. They still do. The night sky was an expanse of unaccountable mystery, an unknowable expanse from which came both life and death, where the imagination could birth the most dreadful beasts. In such a world, the telling of these stories offered solace, for in the act of sharing these terrors, humanity sought to exert a measure of control over its deepest fears.

As civilizations evolved, so did their scary stories. Ancient Greece birthed Medusa. Other cultures had their favorite monsters. The Middle Ages brought with it the Black Death and the fear of eternal damnation. Stories of witches, demons, and cursed relics proliferated, serving as morality tales in a world living with superstitions, and a very real fear of human cruelty. The Renaissance brought forth masters in the works of Edgar Allan Poe, Mary Shelley, and Bram Stoker, timeless tales of terror that continue to engage readers. In the 20th century, the horror genre underwent a profound transformation. The gothic castles and ancient curses gave way to more contemporary horrors. H.P. Lovecraft, Shirly Jackson, Stephen King. Today's stories turn once again on the sense of being out of control in an increasingly hostile and unknowable world. A paradox where "everything knowable is known."

Within these pages, you will find a next generation of emerging writers who embrace these themes and become part of the ongoing evolution of horror. In these tales, you will encounter the restless spirits of the past, the lurking horrors of the present, and the ominous shadows of the future. They are stories that explore the darkness that resides within us all, the fear of the unknown, and the shuddering echoes of our deepest nightmares.

Of course, there are stories of witches, monsters, and devils but also hauntings and resident ghosts. Stories of psychological aberrations; relationships off the rails; misguided hope; strangers and outsiders; cliques and covens and captivity; stormy weather – snow, water, air; the lashing out at so-called authority; revenge.

The authors of these stories each evoke a distinctive style, a unique tone. I especially loved the ethereal darkness evoked by Paula Bryner's *A Traveler Comes By*, and the weather disasters brought to life in Paul Benkendorfer's *A Wendigo of Huron*, and in the breathlessness of Anthony Samuels' *Mayhem on the Mercedes. Dracovich Manor* follows in that same vein. Others paint a normal, if perhaps ho-hum life, such as Stephen Brayton's *The Ritual,* and Michael Roby's *The Decay Diary* - it's anything but. In Joann Schissel's *Night Dance,* isn't there a hint of that eroticism found within the pages of vampire stories?

There have been times in my life – and maybe yours, too - when walking along minding my own business, maybe daydreaming of soon-to-bloom daffodils on a sunny late winter day and then, a corner is turned, the world is changed. Maybe there are now more trees that appear (why?) threatening by their shaded darkness, Maybe the wind changes, or the air pressure, the temperature. Sounds take on alarming meaning. A feeling of being watched. A sudden shiver, a chill, a sense of foreboding, of dread.

These stories all have this, in their own prestidigitations. Some lull with normalcy, even lightheartedness, but some drag the reader right in to that place of fear. There's nothing so engaging: Like driving by a highway wreck. Disturbing yes, but deeply compelling. One cannot - must not - look away.

A Bloody Good Idea
Stephen L. Brayton

Marvin Beeker poked his head into his boss' office. "You wanted to see me, Mr. Gilmore?"

The balding, rotund man behind the immaculate desk pointed to a chair. "Get in here. We need to talk."

Marvin scurried in, closing the door behind him, and slid into the chair. This time, as every time he entered the office, he marveled at the immaculate white walls, sparsely decorated, the white ash hardwood floor, the creamy leather chairs, and the marble white topped desk.

Grayson Gilmore, the magazine publisher, roosted behind the desk like a peeled white potato. He dressed like the Good Humor man and looked like a chunky Colonel Sanders, complete with white goatee.

"Beeker," Grayson grumbled. "This magazine is in trouble."

"Trouble, sir?"

"I said *trouble*."

Marvin squirmed in the chair, his thin frame sliding across the leather up against one of the wooden arms. "How so?"

"For ten years, we've seen excellent sales. However, these last two quarters have been significantly lower. At least fifteen to twenty percent lower."

Marvin pushed fingers through his mop of black hair. He was the magazine's most popular writer. Was he going to be blamed for the drop in sales? What would be the consequences? He'd hate to be let go just as he was forming a new type of story.

"I'm not blaming you," Grayson said. "However, I'm thinking we need a major change in this company."

Marvin swallowed, throat tight and aching. "I'm fired, sir?"

"A change in content, not personnel," Grayson rumbled.

"Yes, sir."

"I'm hearing that people are tired of the same old horror story. They don't want to read the same ghost or haunted house tale."

"I see."

Grayson pursed his fleshy lips and folded his hands on top of his bulging stomach. "That's why I called you in here. We're going to do some brainstorming. I need fresh ideas. No more haunted houses or parts of houses like basements and attics."

"Haunted museums— "

"No haunted museums, sanitariums, hospitals, hotels, prisons, mills or wineries."

"Oh, no," Marvin said. "I thought that haunted winery story from last year was quite nice."

"It's the same old stuff every time. People don't want that any longer." Grayson inhaled a deep breath and narrowed his eyes. "Also, no vampires, werewolves, or any other traditional monster. Especially zombies. I hate them."

Marvin thought about his recent idea but wanted more time to develop it. Instead, he forced his brain into overdrive. "Well, sir, serial killers are always— "

"Nope. No slasher stories. Too pat."

"Hiker finds a video camera in the woods showing the last minutes— "

"Bah!" Grayson ejaculated. "Overdone."

"Alien— "

"And no aliens," Grayson interrupted. "No humans transforming into an alien. No alien monsters on spaceships or earth-like planets."

"Possession?"

"Boring."

"Mutated animals?" Marvin suggested. "Giant spiders— "

"This isn't the 1950s or a schlock cable movie."

"Post-apocalyptic— "

"Trash."

Marvin shifted again in the chair. Grayson narrowed his eyes and stared, waiting. What else was there? "Parasite infection?"

Grayson blew out a snuffling horse type of breath. "No."

"Stalker suspense?"

Grayson shook his head. "And if you say artificial intelligence run amok, you *are* fired."

Marvin closed his mouth. That was his next idea. "I suppose witches, warlocks, evil magicians, and ancient curses are out, too."

"Right. As are any stories dealing with Ouija boards." Grayson slapped the desktop. "Come on, Beeker. You're supposed to be the creative writer. Think of something out of the box, off the wall, out of left field, and those other cliches I don't like."

Marvin scanned the pristine white of the publisher's office. How could the man stand to be in here? Add padding and it easily could be a room for a violent sociopath. Maybe it had affected his mindset. What this room needed was a little...color.

Hmm. Maybe the time had come to present his idea. He had the materials in the trunk of his car. Grayson's secretary was out to lunch. One other writer ensconced in his cubicle, earbuds playing grunge rock that sounded like a compilation of semi-truck crashes.

"Well?" Grayson barked. "Anything? We need something by Thursday." The big man squished his belly against the desk in an attempt to lean forward. "I don't want to have to hire another writer but if you can't step up and produce a winner, I will."

Marvin offered a tentative smile. "Well, sir, I do have an idea for a new type of story."

Grayson leaned back in the chair and turned up a palm. "Spill it."

Marvin sat up straighter, gaining more confidence. "What do people who read horror want?"

"Tell me," Grayson said in a bored tone.

"Reality," Marvin said. "They want to be as close to the story as possible. They want to have the sense they're feeling it personally, experiencing it from the comfort of their recliner or patio swing."

Grayson nodded. "Yes. You're right."

"Let me give it to them." Marvin edged closer to the edge of the chair and leaned forward for emphasis. "I want to write stories about actual, direct experiences of fright and terror."

Grayson frowned. "I don't know what you mean."

"Putting people in real horror situations, then writing about their reactions. If I could see and hear the fear, I know I can recreate those sensations on the page."

Grayson contemplated for ten seconds and nodded. "I think I understand, but not quite. This sounds like something from one of those paranormal shows, where they set up cameras to record the shadow moving across the doorway or the bump in the night. Then you see the wide eyes of the ghost hunters when they think they have solid evidence of the supernatural. Bunch of claptrap, in my opinion.”

“No, no,” Marvin said. “This completely different.” He paused for a breath. *Go for it!* “May I show you, sir? A little demonstration so you can get the idea.”

Grayson inhaled so much air, Marvin feared the room would become a vacuum. Then the big man nodded. “I suppose.”

Marvin hopped out of the chair. “I’ll be back in a minute.”

When he returned, he carried a red plastic tote box which he placed on the chair.

“What this?” Grayson asked.

“Materials for the experiment.” Marvin removed the lid, withdrew a Tablet, switched it to video/audio record, and propped it on the desk, the screen facing his boss. Next, he took out a dispenser for packing tape and walked around the desk. “Just an experiment to give you a taste of my idea.”

“What do you want to do?” Grayson asked.

Marvin removed the seal on the new roll of tape and stretched a short length through the dispenser. “Place your arms on the arms of your chair.”

“Oh, I see.” Grayson chuckled. “So, I can’t get away.”

“Remember, sir, we’re going for realism.”

Another chuckle, but Grayson positioned his arms as instructed. Marvin proceeded to secure both wrists to the chair with packing tape, wrapping the dispenser around and around ten times. He had to make sure the chubby arms couldn’t move. Then he knelt and secured Grayson’s ankles to the front legs of the chair.

Finished, he pressed the *start* button on the Tablet screen to start the recording. “Now, tell me how you feel?””

Grayson winced. “A little uncomfortable. I wish you hadn’t wrapped the tape so tight. What if I have an itch?”

“Any fright or mild terror?”

Grayson wriggled his hefty torso. “No, nothing like that.”

Marvin returned to the box, reached in, and eased out a scalpel? “How about if I show you this?”

“Damn, Beeker. What all you got in there?”

Marvin smiled. “Various implements. Pruning shears, hacksaw, ice pick, but let’s start with this. Tell me what you feel.

Describe what you're experiencing in detail when you see the scalpel."

Grayson gave a nervous laugh. "I, uh, I'm not sure what to say. I didn't expect this."

Marvin held the scalpel with blade pointing up and moved behind Grayson. He reached around the man's bulbous head and placed the tip of the blade an inch from Grayson's left eye. The big man tried to lurch backward. Marvin didn't weight much, but his pressing against the back of the chair combined with Grayson lack of purchase to move, held the chair in place.

"Hey, now," Grayson said. "Careful with that."

"How do you feel now?" Marvin whispered. "Tell me."

"Okay, okay," Grayson said. "I get it. I—I understand what you have in mind for the story. I think we can work with this."

"I know I can." Marvin moved the blade back and forth across Grayson's field of vision. "I envision an ongoing series using all sorts of people. Men, women, all ages, and from every culture, all walks of life, using all sorts of devices. Screwdrivers. Razor blades. Box cutters. Butcher knives. Axes. Needles." He cradled Grayson's head against his chest and gasped in excitement. "Oh, the choices are endless."

Grayson's breaths were quick, producing a sharp whistle with each inhalation. "Yes. Yes."

"You shall be the first story." Marvin caressed the man's face from chin to forehead. "The first case study in terror and horror. Oh, don't you worry about the magazine. I know how to upload the stories, design and submit a cover and can even do the accounting side. You won't even be missed. Neither will your secretary."

"Wait a minute," Grayson said. "Get that thing away from my face. This has gone far enough."

Marvin leaned close to Grayson's ear and whispered, "Oh, no. We're just getting started."

He slashed a deep line down Grayson's cheek, cutting through flesh all the way to the man's gum line. Grayson screamed, but Marvin held the man's head tight against his chest. Red rivulets streamed down this boss' neck, staining the white shirt collar. Drops of crimson speckled the white ash floor.

Marvin's eyes went wide, and he imagined the artwork he could create on the walls and the furniture. Finally, some color in this stark, white room.

He cut a red line behind Grayson's ear from top to lobe.

"Tell me how it feels!" Marvin shouted above Grayson's screeches. The man squirmed but Marvin didn't release him. The Tablet captured every sight, every sound. The blood flowed, and Marvin felt the power of total control surge through him.

"Tell me...*everything!*"

American Gothic
Deb Hannen

Doctor Weiss's first thought when he got off the plane in Cedar Rapids was, "It can't really be like this." Iowa looked uncannily like what he'd imagined. It was as dreamily green and billowy as those paintings by the guy who did American Gothic – Grant Wood, an appropriately bucolic name. As he drove around in a rental car it became increasingly clear that, yes, it really was like this. Everything, the trees, the hills, the clouds, had that iconic plump, firm softness, like a deluxe mattress, and the whole landscape was pieced together in perfect quilt squares of fields.

Doctor Weiss was scouting for offices and apartments, having decided shortly after 9/11 that living on the East Coast was irrational. Ever since he was small, he'd been hearing about his great-grandparents and aunts and cousins who died in Germany. They died for their religion, he was told. They died for their heritage. The obvious thing that nobody ever said, that he had to figure out for himself, was that his ancestors died because they didn't know when to get out. He, David Weiss, was alive today because his grandpa and grandma made what must have seemed at the time like an excessive, irrational decision to sell everything they owned and move halfway across the planet, just because politics were getting ugly in Homburg. He'd wondered about that ever since he was in high school: how do you know when to get out? How do you tell the difference between regular everyday-life craziness and the toxic, lethal kind?

That was what most of his patients came to him to figure out. How do you know when a nice guy who has a temper and drinks a lot passes the tipping point to become an abusive alcoholic? How do you know when to get out? After a decade of schooling and fifteen years of practice, Doctor Weiss had come to the conclusion that you don't know. You can never be sure. All you can do is avoid taking unnecessary risks.

Living in White Plains was an unnecessary risk. He had no particular ties in New York. His mother was safely in Florida. Being a psychiatrist and seeing the aftermath, he'd never wanted a wife or children, any more than ER surgeons want to collect guns. He saw several articles in the journals about the lack of psychiatrists in Iowa. Iowa sounded about right: embedded in the middle of the country, insulated from bombs, Washington, and rising sea levels, like a vital organ with layers of good American fat between it and any bullets.

What Doctor Weiss hadn't realized, besides how cheap everything was here, was how exactly like the movies it would be. The line from that Eighties one, "Is this Heaven? No, it's Iowa." It turned out to be almost true if your idea of heaven was a tranquil one with long distances between towns. One of his Indian expat patients told Doctor Weiss that the heaven of Krishna was called Goloka, which means Cow World. It was a universe of endless green pasture and shady trees, inhabited only by the god and a herd of divine bovines. A blissful place to spend eternity, for people with an unambitious, contented turn of mind. That was what the Midwest was like.

When he set up shop in Cedar Rapids he found, of course, that his clients were pretty much the same as clients in New York. Living in a peaceful place didn't keep them from fighting, cheating, or substance abuse. The one thing that was really different was the secrecy. Instead of thinking of him as another expensive medical specialist, they seemed to think there was something shameful about going to Doctor Weiss. One woman took a taxi to every appointment so nobody would recognize her car. It wasn't so much that they were consciously being deceptive as that they never thought of behaving any other way. Even in session, Doctor Weiss got the feeling that there were a lot of things these people weren't telling him, not because they wouldn't, but because they couldn't.

His current patient, on the other hand, was entirely up-front about his problem. The first thing Jeffrey Holst did at his first appointment was to show the receptionist and Doctor Weiss a picture of his ex.

"If you see this woman, don't let her in. She's stalking me."

"Do you think she could become violent?"

"I don't 'think,' I know. She's dangerous."

"We're very careful about security here," Doctor Weiss said in his best calming voice. "And confidentiality."

Whether or not the man was in actual danger, he was certainly in distress. He looked bad, not just unshaven and poorly groomed from personal crisis, but sick. Jeffrey Holst must be in his mid-forties, but he had that too-skinny, dry look Doctor Weiss associated with the frail elderly, like some vital fluid was evaporating from him. Maybe he was a male anorexic. Prognosis was good as long as you had the sense not to call them anorexics.

Doctor Weiss's next thought, unprofessionally, was that the woman in the picture wasn't attractive enough to put a grown man in that state. She had a pale oval face and a small hard mouth. In fact, after all his study of things Iowan, she looked like the girl in American Gothic.

Doctor Weiss talked the nervous patient into his office and his armchair. (Like everybody else, Jeffrey Holst looked around for a couch first.) He was going to start asking standard questions when he looked at the intake forms on his desk. Doctor Weiss had his second unprofessional reaction of the day. According to his file, Jeffrey Holst was twenty-six. A psychiatrist learns to read people's appearances. Doctor Weiss was sometimes wrong, but not that wrong. It must be a typo.

He said, "You know, people's minds are very sensitive to their bodies. It's hard to be happy when you're hurting. Have you had a medical checkup recently?"

Holst laughed, an abrupt, unfunny laugh. "Three of them. Three different doctors. They all told me to go to you."

While Doctor Weiss was deciding on his next question, his patient said, "I know I look like hell. Don't try to tell me it's not that bad, because it is. It's worse than it looks, even. One of those doctors told me he didn't know what was really wrong with me, but just on the side I've got arthritis and cataracts. I used to play JV ball and now I can't go upstairs without taking a rest. I think I might be going deaf, and my damn hair is falling out."

"Extreme stress . . ."

"That's exactly what all three of them said. It's not stress, it's her."

"The woman in the picture?"

"Her name's Emily. I don't know how, but she's killing me."

"The stalking. Is she actually making threats?

"No, not the stalking. People stalk people all the time. This is something . . . I don't know what she did, but it sucked the life out of me."

"You put so much of yourself and your feelings into the relationship, and then it ended."

"I mean it. That' s not a figure of speech."

Doctor Weiss phrased the next question carefully. "So, you think your ex-girlfriend caused your physical problems directly?"

"You think I'm crazy, don't you?" He stage-laughed again. "Not that you can tell me. I don't know how to explain it so it sounds reasonable, but Emily can really do that. A year ago, when we moved in together, I was fine. Now I'm an old man and she looks better than ever. It's like she fed off me."

A perfectly normal statement, something Doctor Weiss had said himself, as long as it was a metaphor. When somebody was sucking your life out, it meant they were demanding and dependent. If it meant something else, something that could make you age twenty years in one year, that was delusional. Jeffrey Holst was right, of course, and he couldn't say that. He began explaining cognitive-behavior theory to this poor man who really did look half-dead. Holst grasped the idea quickly. He was an intelligent man, which was not necessarily helpful. Someone who's been told all his life that he's dumb learns to trust other people's perceptions. When he develops a delusion, he can sometimes be talked out of it. An intelligent person, who knows that his common sense is usually confirmed by reality, knows better than to listen, and holds on to his belief he's being attacked by vampires.

After work, Doctor Weiss found himself still thinking about Holst. The accepted diagnosis would be conversion disorder. Unacknowledged emotional stress turned into physical illness, like all those sick headaches and strange fits Victorian ladies had, because it was the only way they could express anything negative. But conversion disorder itself was an example of a metaphor slipping into the real world, and it wasn't the only one Doctor Weiss had seen in his practice. There was a seventeen-year-old girl he was treating for depression and self-injuring. Her symptoms improved dramatically as soon as she went to college –

not unusual in itself, but as soon as she got better, all medical hell broke loose in her family. Her father, who was a fitness freak, had a heart attack. Her mother developed some kind of autoimmune disorder that might have been lupus or might have been Lyme disease. Even little brother fell off his bike and cracked his skull. It almost looked as though all that bloodletting the girl did was serving a purpose, acting as an outlet for some deep reservoir of shared pain. When the safety valve shut off, it exploded all over everything.

This was one of those things that everybody knew without anybody talking about it. Every group has them, families, Midwesterners, companies, everybody. The secret for doctors was even in the twenty-first century when they had a firm grasp on how things worked, the human mind and body kept doing things that shouldn't be possible.

The journals had been right about the demand. Doctor Weiss was busy enough to dismiss the subject from his mind, until he saw Holst's ex-girlfriend in the grocery store. Looking over at the next checkout line (grocery stores in Iowa were the size of aircraft hangars) he had another unprofessional thought. How could he ever have found her unattractive? Emily – that was her name, wasn't it? —must be one of those people whose charisma doesn't photograph, because in person she was amazing. She had an unfashionable style of beauty, like the strapping blonde workers in Thirties murals. Again inappropriately, Doctor Weiss thought about the golden Belgian horses he'd seen in a magazine story about the State Fair: creatures as sleek and poised as runway models, but immense and terrifyingly strong, capable of whipping a wagon loaded with rocks around like the hem of a dress. He wondered what her side of the story really was, and what Jeffrey Holst wasn't telling him. It was hard to imagine this person as a shrew or a codependent.

Doctor Weiss watched her check out and wheel her groceries away. Through the glass doors, he saw a car pull up, driven by an elderly man. Her father? He was disappointed when they drove away. Even psychiatrists who know all the symptoms can't get away from fantasy projections.

That Thursday, he tried to get Holst to acknowledge that he himself had some control over his physical well-being.

"I know all that stuff. Drink water and eat a balanced diet. I'm doing all that. I'm pretty healthy for an old man, but I'm not sure it's over."

"Not sure what's over? Your relationship with Emily?"

"I thought maybe you could protect me somehow, if she comes back. But you don't believe me."

"I trust you."

"That's not the same as believing it actually happened. I don't blame you. I didn't believe it either. It took me months for it to even occur to me, which I guess is why . . . why I look like this. I didn't want to believe it. She was so great at first. She was sweet and funny, and she took care of me like a king. But I was so damn sick all the time, and I'd hardly ever been sick before. My teeth hurt. Guys at work thought I was doing meth. That's when I started with the doctors. They didn't have any idea. I didn't figure it out until I had to go to this three-day training in Des Moines. That was the first time I'd gone anywhere without Emily for a month. I'd kind of lost interest in going anywhere. But I felt better as soon as I got to the hotel. By the end of three days, I could read without glasses again. So that was when I knew."

"And what did you do?

"I went home and told her I was moving out. That was bad, especially since she told me I was crazy, too. She got really mad when she couldn't talk me out of it. She said I'd never have a better chance. She asked me if I wanted to be alone if . . .if whatever I had was really serious. You know, if I wasn't going to get better."

"But you are getting better, aren't you?"

"I'm not getting worse, I guess. It seems like she has to be around me physically to do it. That makes me think of all those stories about witches that make people sick and maybe vampires. Everybody believed those kinds of things because people like Emily have always been here."

"Central delusion still firmly in place," Doctor Weiss wrote on his pad. Holst looked better-groomed and less hopeless, but no real progress was being made. Energy parasites. Ordinary-looking people who could be draining you, without your ever knowing. An unpleasant thought. He could understand how it might upset someone who was primed by repressed fears.

That night, Doctor Weiss didn't feel like doing anything but sit on the couch with a book and a mug of tea. He took down <u>The Anatomy of Melancholy</u>. He'd had to read it in college, as one of the founding texts of psychiatry, but he still enjoyed dipping into it at random for weird seventeenth-century lore, like owl-egg omelets to cure alcoholism.

This time the book opened to the chapter on Lovesickness. Old Doc Burton was right alongside the latest literature when he said that sex and relationships were the leading cause of psychological disturbance. The experts would probably not be so happy with the next page.

"The spirits of the air and devils of hell themselves are as much enamored and dote (if I may use that word) as any other creatures whatsoever."

"One Menippus Lycius, a young man twenty-five years of age met such a phantasm in the habit of a fair gentlewoman . . . The young man tarried with her awhile to his great content, and at last married her, to whose wedding, amongst other guests, came Apollonius the philosopher who, by some probable conjectures, found her out to be a serpent, a lamia."

Looking in the glossary, (nobody in these impatient times had a vocabulary like Burton's) Doctor Weiss found that a lamia was a kind of succubus, a snake/woman/spirit who seduced human men to suck their blood.

Lamia. Weird. Another example of the attention principle. Once you start looking for something you'll see it everywhere. Learn a new word, and all of a sudden everybody's saying it. But what kind of "probable conjectures" did you have to have to stand up at a wedding and say, "Stop, don't do it, she's a lamia?" Philosopher in those days meant a scientist, or a wizard, so if anyone would know, he would. In any case, Doctor Weiss thought, it just showed he was too preoccupied with Jeffrey Holst's case. It was a pattern he didn't want to get into, bringing patients' troubles home with him.

That month was busy. For some strange reason three different people who were despondent about their divorces called on the same day, so he was relatively successful getting Holst and Emily out of his head. He should have known it wouldn't last long.

On an impulse, Doctor Weiss bought a book titled <u>Cedar Rapids Then and Now</u> from the Barnes and Nobles where he picked up his <u>Times</u>. He liked the old photographs with hats and oddly shaped cars. He was looking at a picture of a charity banquet from the late 1950's, when he noticed the woman sitting next to the cereal-factory millionaire. She was wearing a flattering Jackie Kennedy dress, but that wasn't what he noticed. She looked familiar. It was Emily.

The back of his neck felt cold. It was nothing, just a funny coincidence, like that picture of Nicholas Cage in the Civil War that people kept posting on the internet.   After all, what were the odds of seeing somebody in a book about Emily's hometown that looked like Emily? Probably it was her great-aunt or something. This was an area of low genetic diversity. He'd noticed it before. On a walk downtown you saw the same pale, blue-eyed oval face repeated dozens of times in different combinations, permutations, genders and ages.

Doctor Weiss was not convinced. He was good at observing people—that was his job. He once treated identical twins and never got them mixed up. This was not someone who looked like Jeffrey Holst's ex, it was the same woman. That was a problem since the caption said 1955. One person couldn't look exactly the same for fifty years.

She could, said a little voice in his head, if she makes someone else get the wrinkles for her. Jeff Holst looked forty. One person can't age twenty years in one year, either.

In his profession, Doctor Weiss disapproved of voices in his head. He wasn't having much luck shutting this one up. Before he could stop it, it said something else disturbing: <u>American Gothic</u>, the painting. Doesn't that woman look like Emily, too? While he was reading up on Iowa, Doctor Weiss got the impression that nobody, even art historians, knew exactly what to make of that painting. They couldn't decide whether it was meant to be affectionate, or cruel satire, or what. Were those people posing proudly in front of their new house, or guarding some horrible ancestral secret inside? And who were they, really? The books said that Grant Wood's models were his sister and his dentist, but the source of that information was the sister herself. Other, more recent books said that Nan Wood was, to put it politely, unreliable about her brother. She consistently covered up or softened the facts about his life that she disapproved of. If she was so sensitive about his being gay, she was bound to disapprove of the brain-twistingly impossible. Besides, the other pictures of perky little Nan don't have the cold, pale, metallic-gold sex appeal of the <u>American Gothic</u> woman.

Doctor Weiss tried to control his hands putting down the picture book. What if people like Emily have always been around? What if there really were lamias? He was unable to stop following the train of thought. If there really were lamias, then life in the early twenty-first century was getting increasingly hard for them. Most people would go to the doctor if they were aging at ten times the normal rate. If you were a lamia, the logical thing to do was stick to places where people, especially men, don't complain or go to doctors.

That poor bastard in the painting was probably a teenager, he thought. Then he took a Lunesta and tried to go to bed. The Lunesta didn't work.

Doctor Weiss managed to keep calm and professional when he actually talked to Jeffrey Holst. "First, do no harm." He couldn't actually reinforce a patient's symptom. That way lay full-blown <u>folie a deux</u>. In college he studied a case where NASA hired a psychiatrist for one of their top engineers. The man was a genius, much too valuable to fire, but his unshakeable belief that he was an alien from another galaxy was becoming a problem in the office. The psychiatrist used all the standard techniques, but the engineer was so completely certain, and he knew so much more about outer-space questions. In the end, the engineer convinced the psychiatrist, not the other way around. So, NASA fired him and decided to put up with the alien engineer. The textbook told it as a humorous cautionary tale, but what if there really had been something strange about the guy? What if he'd had six fingers or something? Then what was the psychiatrist supposed to say?

Jeffrey Holst had plateaued. He wasn't getting any worse, but he wasn't improving either. He seemed to guess that there was something his doctor wasn't telling him. They were circling each other warily in a holding pattern.

In mid-August Holst didn't show up for an appointment. Doctor Weiss left a message on his voicemail, telling himself that people forgot appointments all the time. It didn't necessarily mean anything. The next day, he left another.

On Wednesday, he was just setting up for his first morning patient, when the receptionist came in looking worried.

"Doctor Weiss? She's here."

It was a strange thing that, for all the female patients on his calendar, Doctor Weiss had known immediately who "she" was.

"That woman he told us not to let in."

"It's all right. I want to talk to her."

She was wearing a black suit that made her skin and hair paler. Doctor Weiss could feel the pull of her power, like gravity.

She closed the door. "I thought I should tell you, since you were his doctor. Jeffrey passed away on Saturday."

"'Passed away?' You killed him."

"I didn't want to. I really thought I was going to let him go, this time. If he'd just stayed away." She had a beautiful soft, low voice. An excellent thing in woman, even one who's not a human woman.

"You killed him and <u>ate</u> him. You eat people."

"Everything eats people. Jobs do, countries do. Why don't I have as much right to exist as them? I don't enjoy being a monster, you know. I do what I have to do. That's why I'm asking you not to tell anybody about me."

"And why would I do what you're asking?

"It's as much for your sake as mine. Do you know what would happen to a psychiatrist who went around telling people his client was killed by an energy parasite in the form of a woman?"

Doctor Weiss did. At best, he'd lose his practice and his new home. At worst . . . Doctor Weiss knew enough about the mental health system to decide that he was never going to enter it as a patient. He'd settled long ago that if he diagnosed himself with dementia or any of the major thought disorders, he'd prescribe a bottle of Oxycontin. You have to know when to get out. You have to know when a heroic gesture is worth anything at all and when evil will just roll over you and never even notice.

"We understand each other, then. You won't see me again. I've been here too long and gotten careless. It's time to move."

Even while he was shaking and sick with fear, some part of him was sad to be left by this woman who shimmered like the mirage-water on a highway.

She didn't disappear. She walked out of the office like everybody else. He heard her say "You, too," when Sandy told her "Have a nice day."

There are probably others like her, he thought. I'll leave the Midwest. Doctor Weiss knew that he wasn't going to. He could spend the rest of his life scurrying around the country, shooed from place after place by terrorists, cancer clusters and real, literal monsters. It was important to know when to get out, but it was also important to know when there was no out to get.

That was the true other face of this peaceful green place. It wasn't so much that the peace was a disguise, and the people were all hypocrites covering up dirty secrets. No, the thing he should have seen from the first is that peaceful, wholesome places are dangerous because the predators are right there in plain sight and you don't recognize them.

He, Leo Weiss, must belong here now, because now he had a true Midwestern-style secret: not the kind that you won't tell, but the kind that you can't.

Inside Me
Cordelia Kelly

Derek scrubbed his palms along his pants as he approached the girl filling her backpack at her locker. "Hey, Chelsea."

Chelsea stood to face him, her amber curls swinging over her shoulder. As always, he felt a shock when facing her. Chelsea Holden was the girl of his dreams. The girl of everyone's dreams. He couldn't mess it up now; this was his shot.

"Hey Derek, what's going on?"

"Um, good. I mean, nothing." He ran his hand through his hair, then dropped it, trying not to fidget. "I uh, I was wondering if you wanted to go to a movie with me sometime." He said it too fast and cursed himself.

Chelsea hugged her book to her chest. "Like on a date?" Her nose wrinkled ever so slightly. At his fumbling silence, she bit her lip and nodded her head.

"Listen, Derek, it's so nice of you to ask. But I broke up with Ryan, like, five minutes ago. And I'm looking to just be single for a little bit. So, thanks for thinking of me, but I just want to be friends, okay?"

She smiled wide and with a toss of her hair, she left Derek behind in a cloud of perfume.

"Uh, right, okay." Derek spoke too late, as she was already gone. He ran his fingers through his hair again, spinning when he heard a giggle. Nobody was looking his way, but he was sure they were laughing at him. "Bitch." His whisper was barely audible.

He stormed down the hallway. A flash of black hair disappearing down a hallway ahead of him gave him pause. Then his mouth twisted into a half smile.

He jogged forward and grabbed the girl's arm before she went into her classroom.

"Hey!" She spun and pushed him hard. "Derek, what the hell?"

"Louise." Now that he had her attention, he slouched back against the lockers. "I need you to do something for me."

"And from your manhandling of my person, the chances of that happening are slim to none." Louise rolled her eyes, turning to go.

"You're a witch, right?"

Louise stopped in her tracks and twisted back to him, condescension dripping from her dark lip sticked smile. "A girl dyes her hair and paints her fingernails, and all of a sudden, she's a witch? You have absolutely no imagination."

"You mean this whole goth vibe you have going on here? It makes me wonder if you're hiding in plain sight. Because I remember you used to be into some freaky things. You could make things happen if you wanted to. Witchy things."

She shook her head, her hair falling over one eye. "People can say all sorts of things. That doesn't make it true." She eyed him. "What kind of witchy thing are you looking to have happen? Are you haunted by the ghost of poor fashion choices? I could probably exorcise it, but you'd have to burn all your clothes."

Derek's lip curled. "Make Chelsea Holden fall in love with me."

Louise's thin eyebrows arched nearly to her hairline, and she let out a staccato burst of laughter. "Chelsea Holden, Little Miss Perfect? You don't need witchcraft, Derek, you need an apocalypse."

The bell rang and she turned back to class, but his low poisonous voice stopped her.

"People talk, you know, and sometimes they can even prove what they're saying. For instance, I heard that you're freaky, not just in a bride of Satan way. Rick was running his mouth about some time he's spent with you. He has photos to back it up." His gaze raked over her body. "I wouldn't have expected you to wear pink under all that."

Louise's pale cheeks went whiter still and her eyes darkened. She glanced over her shoulder at her classroom, then grabbed him by the front of his shirt and pulled him into an alcove, shoving him against the wall by his throat. He was much larger than her but she had surprised him. Black-tipped nails dug into his skin.

"Derek, you miserable little prick. What do I care if you've seen photos of me, other than you're a dirty perv."

"It's video too." He strained against the pressure on his windpipe. "Good stuff, you look good. I figured you've got this whole perfect GPA thing going for you. You probably don't want a sex tape scandal following you to college. Do one little favour for me and nobody else has to see it."

"He's shared it?" She released him.

"No." Derek shrugged, rubbing at the marks on his throat. "But I could hack him no problem. Rick is an idiot."

"Fuck." Louise dragged her hair out of her face. "Derek, I can't make Chelsea Holden fall in love with you. It simply isn't possible. People's emotions can't be controlled like that. It doesn't help that you're a despicable excuse for a human being."

"Love, whatever. You can make her want me, can't you? That's just hormones. You could do that for me."

"You don't understand. Playing with lust, it's not just unstable, it's dangerous. It's not something to mess with."

"I think I can handle it. Now, why don't you be a good little witch and give me what I want. Then I'll take care of you."

Derek's smirk dropped when Louise's eyes shone unnaturally bright. He balled his hands into fists, steeling himself from taking a step back.

"You'll find I rarely need to be taken care of. I'll give you what you're asking for. If you understand I'm not responsible if things don't go the way you planned." She let out a shuddering breath and left without a backwards glance. "I'll text you."

* * *

How dare he threaten her like that?

Louise stood in her kitchen, her palms pressing into the counter to control her trembling. The vulgarity of his threats, the violence of it, made her queasy. Derek wasn't the boy he used to be.

She shook out her fingers. If she was going to cave to his blackmail, she would have to get working. A lust spell was no easy thing to create, although being a teenager gave her an advantage. Her high school was so full of horny thoughts she could practically bottle the air.

31

It was specificity, though, that gave it potency. How would she get Chelsea Holden to fall for Derek White? He wasn't unattractive but they weren't in the same league. Chelsea, a straight-A student and sometimes model, had just broken up with the captain of the hockey team. They were high school royalty and would be back together by the end of the week.

Derek was most likely to be found under the bleachers, stoned out of his mind. The direction he was going, he had no future to speak of. Whereas Chelsea was so full of bright promise, she glowed with it.

Louise clenched her fists, allowing the nails to bite into the skin. They had been friends once, her and Derek. They would watch horror movies together, giggling at the scariest parts and throwing popcorn at the screen. She loved spending time at his home, with his perfectly ordinary family.

But he had grown beyond scary movies, and her, and if she had wanted to be more than friends at a certain point in the past, he had made sure she knew he would never be interested. It was calculated cruelty that he asked this of her.

"Dammit, Derek." The problem was, she could make this potion. She had all the ingredients, including the one crucial element that would make it extremely potent. But could she do that to Chelsea? The girl was nice enough, so high in the popularity stratosphere she didn't even need to be mean. She didn't deserve to be forced to want someone against her will.

But a few drops might be enough to open Chelsea up to the idea of Derek. Not enough for persuasion, not enough that she couldn't say no, but she might give him a second thought. Louise tapped her nails against the counter in an uncertain tattoo. She should have never hooked up with Rick, he really was a moron, and she was a moron for not ensuring he wasn't taping her. Were all the boys in her school perverts?

Sighing, Louise opened her mom's liquor cabinet. On one side was an array of near-empty bottles; on the other was a tray of her own supplies. She had told her mother she was really into essential oils; her mom had responded with a shrug.

She flipped through her phone to a file where she kept most of her spells. She swiped open the recipe labelled No. 9 and read the ingredients. Rose water, cloves, rosemary and distilled water infused with rose quartz.

It was basic stuff, the foundation for a romantic love spell. Those feelings were superficial and hovered close to the surface, easy to nudge out into the open. One by one she added them to a clean jar.

But the most essential ingredient, the element that would ensure the potion worked as it should, could not be found at an Etsy shop. Louise took out a clean kitchen knife and sliced it across the pad of her thumb. As the blood welled up, she thought of how she used to feel for Derek, of throwing popcorn at him and laughing hysterically, back when he had been kind. Blood of one who wanted the object of the spell.

She murmured words of intent, feeling the swirling energy of lust and enchantment funnel through her. Three drops fell into the vial. She watched as the dark liquid spread out like jellyfish before dissolving.

She texted Derek: *It's done. You better hold up your end of the bargain.*

He was at her house within the hour. She let him in, self-conscious. He had never been to her house before; they would always hang out at his. He took in the dirty front entrance, then his gaze flicked to hers.

"So? What are we waiting for?"

Louise clicked her tongue. "Without patience, there can be no genius." She murmured the quote as she looked him up and down. "Obviously."

"Fuck you." By the nervous darting of his gaze, Louise could tell she made him uncomfortable. Her lips curved into a smile.

"What's wrong, Derek, scared to enter a witch's lair?"

"I just want to get away from you." He growled the words, and they stung more than she would admit. She held out a vial of the potion, only a tiny fraction of what she had made. The herbs having been strained out, it was a clear, pinkish liquid. Before Derek could grab it, she withdrew her hand, holding it away from him.

"What guarantee do I have that you'll get rid of the sex tape?"

Derek stared at her, eyes narrowing to slits. "It's already done. I didn't like the thought of Rick having that tape, so I got rid of it."

A well of warmth stirred in Louise's chest, but she made herself scowl. "You lied to me."

"Not exactly. I kept a copy for myself." He grinned, wolfish.

The warmth curdled in her stomach. "You're disgusting."

He held out an open hand. "Just give me what I need."

"What you need is industrial-level therapy." She pressed the tiny vial into his hand. "Dilute this. We're done here."

"Like hell we are." Derek squinted at the trace of pink liquid. "There's only a drop here."

"Three drops in her drink, Derek, it's enough to get her to look at you twice. You'll have to do the rest with your winning personality, and it's more than you deserve."

He grabbed Louise before she could slam the door in his face. "I told you I wanted her to want me. Really want me, like in my bed."

"I won't let you rape her." Louise hissed as she tried to twist out of his grasp.

"It's not rape if she comes willingly."

"You have a fucked-up idea of consent. Let me go."

"Give me more or I'll send out that video to every single person in this town."

Tears filled her eyes. "I don't care. I won't give you the rest."

Derek's eyes flashed with triumph. "So, there is more." He shoved past Louise into her house, as she tried to grab at his arms. He swatted her away and approached the residue of her shellwork laid out on the counter. In the middle was the potion, muddy with herbs and blood.

Derek snatched it from the counter as Louise tried to wrestle it out of his grasp. She stumbled as he shrugged her off.

"You don't understand. Love potions are dangerous. It won't work the way you want."

"I think you just don't want it to work, right? Thanks for this, you freak."

Louise chased after him into the street, but he was already pedalling away and she wouldn't be able to catch him in time. She spun back to her house, fuming.

*   *   *

Louise arrived at Carrie Watson's party late, surveying the scene for potential disasters. Everything seemed normal. Kids sprawled across the lawn, chatting and sipping from solo cups while music blared. No screaming, which was a good sign.

Carrie's house was far nicer than the row housing Louise grew up in, and the backyard rolled down into the ravine beyond. She picked her way through people sprawled on the front steps. Some of the partygoers side-eyed her, wondering why she was there. This wasn't her crowd.

Louise mingled, uneasy. She had never fit in at their school, counted down the days before she could leave. She survived by keeping her head down and staying out of the spotlight. It had taken her hours to figure out where Chelsea would be tonight. Finally, her chem partner gave her reliable information that anybody who was somebody would be at Carrie Watson's house tonight, and Chelsea Holden was certainly someone.

Louise didn't see her after a few walk-throughs, and her panic mounted. If Derek had given Chelsea all of the potion, she could be poisoned. And that was best-case scenario.

Finally, Louise marched up to Carrie Watson and asked if she'd seen Chelsea. Carrie seemed mildly offended Louise spoke to her. "On the back porch with Derek White. She was all over him." She snorted, fuzzy with alcohol. "Weird night for randoms."

"You have no idea." Louise blew silky dust into Carrie's face. "Forget what you saw. Forget Chelsea was here, and forget I was here."

By the time Carrie had finished spluttering, Louise was already gone.

*   *   *

Chelsea gazed up at Derek. Her eyes were so blue, and she was looking right at him. Finally seeing him, just like he had always imagined.

The air outside was cool, but he could feel the heat rising from her body. It hadn't taken must convincing for her to drink the martini he'd made for her, the pink potion swirled in vodka. Derek leaned into Chelsea, and she mirrored his gesture. Smirking, he lifted her hair to whisper in her ear. "Let's go somewhere."

She giggled and rose to her feet, clinging to his hand, fingers entwined with his. Derek pulled her towards the house, but she stopped, shaking her head.

"No, this way." She tugged Derek off the patio, down the sprawling lawns towards the ravine.

"Wait, stop." Derek was half-laughing, half-annoyed as Chelsea dragged him away from the others. Down in the trees that surrounded the creek, the air was humid and chilled. There was no sign of manicured lawn, nothing but swampy land left to grow wild. This wasn't how he had pictured it. He had wanted to stay at the party; wanted everyone to see him with Chelsea. "Where are we going? Let's get back up to the party."

"Derek." Chelsea said his name like an incantation. Her eyes were wide and dilated dark. "I want you inside me."

Lust hit him like a hammer, but still, he hesitated. "Yeah. But let's find a nice bed somewhere?"

"I can't wait." Chelsea lunged for him, fighting his jacket off him. Once more he found himself laughing, but it wasn't funny.

"Hang on. No need to rush."

"Yes, I need you inside me. Now." She grabbed the back of his neck and dragged him forward. Her greedy lips grabbed his, and she kissed him with a strength he didn't understand. He couldn't breathe and shoved her off.

"I want you too, Chelsea, just give me a minute."

Her eyes were empty and hollow, no longer seeing him as she grappled at his clothes, bringing him close again. "I need you. I need you inside me."

Derek tried to push her away but tripped over a root behind him. He fell to the ground with a squelch, mud from the ravine splashing over his legs. "What the hell is wrong with you?"

Chelsea didn't seem to mind the filth. She leapt on top of Derek, straddling him as her knees sank into the muck. She ripped his t-shirt from his body. "Need you. Need you. Need you."

"No, stop it. I don't want this." His voice rose higher as he scrambled to get away from the frenzied girl, but she kept dragging him back, her fingers clawed.

"Get off of me." Derek reeled back and punched Chelsea in the face. Her head snapped back, but it barely slowed her down. She crawled up his body.

"Need you, need you, need you inside me." Her gripping hands went to his throat, holding him in place as he writhed underneath her in horror. With her staring eyes, covered in mud and blood, she looked nothing like the sweet girl he'd wanted to possess.

He screamed and kept on screaming as she lowered her mouth to his neck and ripped out a chunk of flesh.

*   *   *

Several of the kids sitting around the keg laughed, heads tucked together to discuss the gossip when Louise joined the group. "What the hell got into Chelsea? Is she doing community service?"

"What's going on?" she asked. The guy sitting next to her blinked blearily, then leaned in. "Chelsea Holden basically attacked Derek White and dragged him to the river. It was wild."

"Shit," Louise said.

"What?"

"Nothing." Louise reached deep into her pockets and threw a cloud of dust into the air. She blew through pursed lips, causing the powder to whirl around the patio, then out further to consume the entire house. "Forget what you saw, forget I was here, forget Chelsea was here."

Everyone started to cough and jump to their feet, looking around in confusion. Louise's voice resonated with power. "You're having the night of your life. One you'll barely remember."

There were shouts and barks of laughter, and the music inside increased in volume.

Louise sprinted down the lawn to the ravine, hoping she wasn't too late.

When the screams started, she knew she was.

Louise followed the howls of pain, pressure building behind her eyeballs as she pressed forward through the foliage. She was nearly there when the screams became moans, then faded to an obscene gurgling.

She whipped around a gnarled trunk to find the ghastly scene. Derek's neck and chest were ripped apart. His eyes were wide, his mouth twisted in a silent scream.

As Louise approached, Chelsea raised her face and gave a beatific smile. Her face was smeared with gore. "It's so good," she said. "I needed him inside me."

Tears spilled over Louise's cheeks as she nodded. "I know you did. But you have to come with me now."

"I needed him," Chelsea said again but allowed Louise to lead her like a child. They made their way down to the creek, where Louise splashed water on Chelsea to get most of the blood off. Her eyes were closed, her face soft. "It feels so good."

"I know it does." Louise's voice was choked. "You need to get out of those ruined clothes, okay? I have some here." She rummaged through her bag, finding her change of gym clothes. "Just put these on, okay? I'll take your ruined things."

Chelsea was compliant as a doll, satiated by the night's magic and feasting, and followed directions without a complaint. While she changed, Louise went back to Derek's body.

"You idiot," she whispered, stifling her sobs as she inched his body further into the creek until it was partly submerged. She hoped he would start to decompose quickly, to destroy any evidence of what had truly happened.

Dressed in Louise's too-short gym clothes, Chelsea followed her through the ravine. They took a winding path, avoiding the party as they made their way down the street to her car. Driving as fast as she felt she could get away with, it took Louise several attempts to figure out where Chelsea lived, as Chelsea wasn't doing much but rubbing her face and laughing. Finally, Louise pulled up in front of the modest bungalow where she lived with her mother.

Chelsea paused when the car stopped, her eyebrows furrowing. "Louise? What's going on? I feel ..."

"Everything is fine. You are going to go inside and have a shower, washing your hair thoroughly. You hit your face on a cabinet and decided to stay in and watch movies with your mom."

Chelsea nodded uncertainly and sat still. Louise had to come around to the passenger seat and tugged Chelsea out of the car, bringing her up to the front door.

Chelsea's mom came to the door and drew back in horror at the blood still smudging her daughter. "What happened to her?"

"She's fine, Mrs. Holden. Chelsea just needs to go upstairs and have a shower."

"But …" Mrs. Holden went to follow her daughter, who moved dreamlike towards the back of the house, but Louise grabbed her hand. She blew the last of her powder gently into her face.

"Chelsea had an accident and hit her face on a cabinet. She decided to stay home with you and watch movies all night."

"I … right. What?"

"I was never here." Louise backed down the steps. Mrs. Holden blinked in confusion before she shut the door with a shrug. Louise sagged in relief.

She drove down to the dumpsters that lined the warehouses on the other side of town. There she stuffed Chelsea's sodden mess of clothing she had worn to the party, deep where they wouldn't be found. Then she made her way home, crying the whole time.

* * *

"Oh my god, Chelsea, did you hear what happened?"

Chelsea turned to face her friend Desiree, eyes clear and smiling. "What?"

Louise lounged against a locker nearby, watching her. It was Monday morning. She'd spent the entire weekend on high alert, trying to figure out who knew what.

Desiree leaned in, lowering her voice. "You know Derek White? Apparently, he *died* at Carrie Matson's party Friday night. His parents reported him missing after the party, and they found his body down in the ravine. It looked like he had been ripped apart by wild animals."

39

Chelsea spun on Desiree, her eyes huge. "That is insane! Poor Derek. Do you know he asked me out last week?"

"He actually asked you out?" Desiree gave a scathing laugh before realizing how inappropriate it was and cleared her throat. "It's crazy that he was so alive last week, and now he's gone. Savaged, apparently."

Chelsea looked downcast. "Shit, that's terrible. What kind of wild animals even live in the ravine?"

Desiree shrugged. "Rabid coyotes? I won't be going near there anytime soon. Where were you, by the way? I thought we were going to meet at Carrie's."

Chelsea's face went blank, and Louise held her breath. Then Chelsea let out a little laugh. "I was such a ditz and ran into the door of a cabinet." She showed a faint bruise on her cheek, barely visible. "It looked worse before. I decided to just stay in and watch movies with my mom. It ended up being fun."

"Huh, weird." Desiree inspected her cheek. "You can barely see it now. Actually, what have you been doing? New skin routine? You are absolutely glowing!"

Chelsea's face stretched into a wide grin. "I think it's just taking some time off from partying. I feel so good and … I don't know, satisfied for some reason."

Desiree's look was contemplative. "Maybe I'll take some time off from partying too if I can look like that."

"Good idea." Chelsea hooked her arm through her friend's, and they made their way down the hallway. "Let's just hang out next weekend."

They passed Louise in the hallway. Satisfied Chelsea was okay, she pushed off the lockers and caught Desiree's notice.

"Goth girl," she said under her breath but still loud enough to be overheard. "She is so weird."

Chelsea glanced back over her shoulder, and her grin stretched even wider. She caught Louise's gaze. "I don't know. I think she's kind of cool."

And then she winked.

Night Dance
Joann Schissel

Miriam opens her eyes and pulls herself up from the twin-sized mattress on the floor. The room is windowless. A single light bulb, encased in a metal cage, hangs centered on the low ceiling. Pallid light casts shadows on the cinder block walls. An old camp toilet hugs the corner.

The smell of mildew and urine reeks in the chilled air, and she draws the rough wool blanket tighter around her quivering shoulders. Her mind blurs with confusion.

Weak and wobbly, she struggles to stand on the cold cement. *Must find a way out.* A metal slab cleaves into the surrounding monotony of rough, gray walls. It may be a door, but it has no handles.

Leaning against the wall, she stumbles forward and hammers her fists against cold steel. "Let me out!"

Tracing her fingers along the wall, she paces the perimeter of the room — four steps wide, six steps long. Over and over the process is repeated. Her breath labors as if the room itself is tightening a fist around her lungs.

A man's muffled voice comes from the other side of the door. "Are you ready to be good?"

Her shaking palms press against the steel. "Who are you? What do you want? Please… let me out!"

A bowl slides through a flap at the bottom of the door. The opening is no bigger than a mail slot and it clanks shut. Brownish-tinted liquid sloshes inside the bowl. Her mouth is dry and her throat screams for water, so she slurps it up.

The room spins and the light extinguishes, drowning her in an ebony sea. Her skin prickles with the sensation of another presence nearby and she huddles in a corner.

A spark of blue luminescence hovers and expands above her. A rounded face, pale as a winter moon stares at her with translucent eyes shimmering like watery milk.

The apparition's features are terrifying, but Miriam can't escape the locked hold it has on her. "You're not real…go away!"

Wisps of white hair flutter over a tattooed shape forming a third eye in the center of the specter's forehead. The eye's jet-black chasm spirals with dimension, and Miriam fights the pull as if falling into a tunnel. Blue lips open. "Miriam, are you ready for death?" The female voice resonates with mesmerizing tones offering a release from suffering.

Miriam recoils, pressing hard against the wall. Her body convulses with fear.

"No! I want to live." Weeping like a child, she squeezes her eyes shut.

"Then you must do what I tell you. To save yourself."

Miriam opens her eyes but she may have well been blind. The apparition has disappeared. Only the voice remains, whispering in her ear.

"You're a foolish whore. So easy to entice into the house with the promise of money. He's a murderer, you know, my husband Benedict. I spend eternity feeling his hands crushing my throat until I relinquished all breath. He'll forget you exist here, until one day he smells your rotting corpse in his secret room."

Miriam clamps her palms over her ears, yet the ghostly voice remains louder than ever.

"Tell him Elisa is here. If you want to live you must do as I say."

The bulb flickers on. Even though the light is dim, she squints. Her fingers explore her face. Dry and powdery texture mixes with sweat. Hair cropped so short, she can't see its color. The skin around her jaw sags somewhat but the back of her hand is smooth. A plain gold band encircles her left ring finger. There are no injuries, no pain, no memory. The long cotton dress she wears has a pattern of faded red hearts and she draws her knees up under the skirt, hugging them tight against her chest.

The slot slides open from the door with no handles. This time it is different. Eye-level. She can't tell if he is watching her.

"What's your name?" he asks.

She uncoils and drags herself toward his voice. "My name is Miriam. Please, sir, please… let me go. I won't tell anyone."

Her pleading is met with silence except for the scraping of metal when the slide closes.

"Elisa is here too," she raises her tenor in desperation, pressing against the door and holds her breath to listen.

"How do you know Elisa?"

"Elisa wants you to know she is here," Miriam repeats.

He says nothing but shoves something through the bottom slot. A chunk of bread. She tears a bite, but her throat is so dry she can't swallow. The light goes out and darkness returns.

The whispers begin again, rushing in her ears. "You have him interested but my husband is a cruel man. You must appeal to his appetites. Tell him to bring you Elisa's black lace and you will dance for him tonight." The whisper fades into the dark.

There is no sense of time. Only lightbulb on, lightbulb off. When the cell illuminates again, a bowl of broth and a small bottle of water appears through the slot. Her limbs are feeble, but she manages to crawl to the door. She soaks the dry bread into the liquid and consumes the contents with greed. When every morsel of food and drop of water is gone, she leans against the door, hoping he is still on the other side.

"Benedict, bring me Elisa's black lace. I will dance for you tonight." She doesn't know if he hears her frail voice. If he has, he doesn't ask how she knows his name. The light remains on. Six times she paces the perimeter path, fearing he won't return and she'll die here.

The door slot opens and a black bundle is pushed into the room.

She retrieves the fabric. It is fashioned like a bathing suit. The lace stitched around the low-cut neckline is coarse and scratchy. She sheds the long dress in exchange for the laced bodice, molding her into its ridged contours with plastic wires. The top of her breasts is exposed and compressed together in an uplift, allowing only shallow breath. Long sleeves cover her arms. Something stiff digs into the flesh of her wrist.

"Yes, that will be perfect," the ghost voice purrs. "You must dance until you can't stand upright anymore. That's when he will punish you with a whip."

Miriam sucks in a whimper.

"But that is what the vial is for," Elisa hisses. "My plan was perfect, but he strangled me before I could use the potion."

Miriam fumbles with the small tube sewn into a pocket inside the sleeve.

"Add two drops into his drink. You must do this quickly, before the dance, so he falls asleep. That's when you can escape. If you fail in any part of this task like I did, you'll end up buried beside me under the room."

Miriam waits, lying straight on the mattress, the only position that relieves the needling from the costume's wires. She practices removing the vial with one hand. It slips from her fingers with each attempt.

"Are you ready to be good?" The man's voice outside the door startles her.

"Yes, I'll be good."

"Lay on the mattress, stomach down. Keep your eyes closed."

She follows his commands. The door unlocks and creaks open. The odor of sweat overpowers the other putrid smells in the room. His touch on her back frightens her and she grimaces. Silken fabric is wrapped around her head covering her eyes and he pulls her to standing, never removing his hold on her arm. He guides her and she complies — step up here, again, again, turn here. The air becomes warmer and smells of cigars and spice. Old-fashioned music plays a melancholy song by some long-dead crooner. The tune becomes louder as she is led forward.

"Stop here," he orders. He releases her arm. His breath heats the back of her neck. The blindfold is untied and slips across her bare shoulder onto the floor.

Her vision blurs and she blinks to refocus. Light flickers from a dozen candles casting animated shadows within the sparse room. A single upholstered chair is placed in the center. Beside it, a small table holding a glass of amber liquid wafting the scent of alcohol.

"Stand still, I want to look at you."

Miriam freezes in place. He steps around her and unbuttons his blazer before lowering himself into the chair. His face is haggard, lined with wrinkles. Oiled gray hair tucks behind his ears. He grasps the highball glass with hands speckled by age spots and takes a drink.

"Come closer." He beckons her with a hand motion.

She stands in front of him. He reaches out and draws her against him, closing his eyes and burying his head between the cleavage of her breasts.

The vial loosens from the small pocket into her hand. Trembling, she adds the drops to his drink, nearly missing the glass. The vial rolls in her palm and slips between her fingers onto the carpeted floor. Her heartbeat pounds in her ears.

He tilts his head in the direction where it fell and narrows his eyes.

"I want to be good," she blurts out. With a brush of her fingertips along his chin, his gaze is redirected back to her. The words taste bitter, and she swallows her disgust.

He leans back into the plush cushion of the wing chair and takes a long swig of the whiskey without taking his eyes off her. His expression remains emotionless as if he is studying prey.

Bowing her head, she falls to her knees, pressing her cheek onto his lap. Her arms drape in submission onto the floor. "I will do what you want," she says without flinching.

Her fingers search until she finds the vial and pushes it underneath the skirt of the chair.

Ice rattles in the glass.

He sighs and touches the back of her neck, frigid fingers wrapping around delicate skin. "You've returned to me, Elisa. We can be happy again."

Miriam wrenches free from his grasp and sits back with her hands on his knees. "Benedict, I'm Mariam. You have to release me now." Her eyes dart to the empty glass on the table and back to him.

For the first time, a weak smile crosses his lips. He caresses her cheek. "Elisa, darling, your delusions change you into someone else. This episode was especially frightful. I had to lock you in the room to keep you safe…to keep both of us safe."

Miriam backs an arm's length away from him. "I don't understand what you're talking about. You kidnapped me."

Benedict shakes his head with wide eyes. "The demon inside you needed to be starved out. Don't you see? They would take you away from me and put you into an asylum if they knew about your insanity."

He leans forward, scratching his hand across his throat. Beads of sweat sprout on his forehead. "Darling, you're not Miriam. Don't you remember? Miriam was the girl you strangled in a jealous rage. You called her a whore because you thought I had an affair with her." His words sputter out and slur.

"Miriam meant nothing to me." He staggers toward her, gasping. "I didn't want you to go to prison. That's why I buried her under the room. No one would ever find out."

He grabs his throat, choking, and crumples to the floor. "It's you I love, Elisa."

Eyes roll back in his head, and he plummets to the floor.

Miriam stares at his motionless body several minutes before creeping over to him, resting her ear on his chest until his heartbeat ceases. With a gentle touch, she closes his eyes, hiding the dilated pupils. Candles flicker out and the soft music stops. She rises and peels off the black costume leaving her naked and walks toward a wall mirror. Beside the mirror is a photo of a younger-looking Benedict next to a smiling woman with short, dark hair, wearing a long dress patterned with bright red hearts.

She stares at the face reflected in the mirror. Her finger traces the tattoo of a third eye in the center of her forehead.

Dream State
Romana Tamm

1

"I can't believe it, Bob!" Bob Haskin's landlady clutched his arm, body shaking with excitement.

Bob had just stepped out of the apartment building on the way to his car when Agnes Birch rushed up to him from her first-floor unit down the hall. He wasn't in any danger of being late for work but knew if he didn't catch the light at Second, he'd have to wait at least ten minutes for the train three blocks farther on to pass. However, he couldn't be rude. His landlady was a sweet ole gal.

"What happened, Agnes?" he asked. "Did the Fareway run out of butter pecan ice cream?"

Agnes rippled off waves of laughter. "No, silly. It was my dream."

"Your...dream?"

"My dream," she repeated. "Oh, I had to tell someone this morning. I knew you'd be leaving for work, and I promise not to keep you too long, but..."

Again, her five-two frame quivered like she'd drunk an entire four pack of Red Bull for breakfast. Bob sighed. What the heck, he thought, he could spend the time at the tracks answering email on his phone. "What about your dream?"

Agnes took a deep breath and launched into her story. "I've had this same dream for almost a week now. I mean, the exact same dream. About Mary Ellen. Do you know her?"

"I don't think so?"

"Well, you wouldn't, I guess," she said. "Mary used to be my best friend. We've known each other since high school. Anyway, about ten years ago, we got into a fight. Not a fistfight, just, oh, you know, a little tiff."

"About what?"

"She said I had won the blue ribbon at the fair only because I stole her gooseberry jam recipe. She was so upset she tripped on the steps, fell, and sprained her ankle."

"You pushed her, didn't you?" Bob said with a smile.

Another peal of laughter. "Of course, I didn't. Anyway, she blamed me and refused to speak to me ever again. We just kind of drifted apart after that. Until yesterday."

"What happened yesterday?"

"The dream. Like I said, I've had the same dream for a week. I see Mary in the beauty shop after all these years, and we start talking and she apologizes for accusing me of stealing her recipe. We make up and become friends again."

"That's what you dreamed about?"

"Yes," she said, her voice rising. "And then yesterday, it happened."

"What happened?" Bob asked. Sometimes waiting for Agnes to get to the point in her stories was like waiting for the doctor after the nurse leaves the room after checking all the vitals.

"I went into Ruby's Salon and who do you think I see?"

"Ruby?"

"Oh, stop it, now. Mary, of course. And we had the same conversation we had in my dream. Turns out, she had been having the same dream as mine. The same exact dream. Isn't that wild? I mean isn't that bizarre?"

2

Bob sat in his car, the rhythm of the train cars over the wooden crossing playing in the background to his thoughts. Agnes' report on her dream was bizarre, but it wasn't the first of this kind of tale he'd heard. Only a week ago, a coworker shared a similar story during the lunch hour. How he had dreamed the same scene for four nights straight about a friend, subsequently met the friend, and discovered he, too had had the same dream. They'd had a conflict which was then resolved.

Bob recalled also, a small article in the paper not long back, that this type of thing was happening elsewhere in the country. Maybe a half dozen cases so far.

He had congratulated his landlady for the reconciliation with her friend, but internally, he shivered, uneasy. His wasn't excitement, but a surreal sense of unease. Could something be happening to certain pairs of people? Some psychic phenomena? He didn't know…

…but it rushed to the forefront of his thoughts because he'd had a recurring dream the last three nights. One that involved Jennifer.

He hadn't stolen a jam recipe from his former fiancé. No, he'd done much worse. One night, he'd gotten drunk with some friends and woke up with a stranger. Granted, the woman was attractive, but she wasn't Jennifer. His fiancé caught them together when she stopped by to take him out for breakfast. There had been anger and tears and her flinging the engagement ring into the sewer.

They hadn't spoken in almost two years.

The first time he had the dream, Bob hadn't thought anything of it. The scene was never going to happen, so why be concerned. After the second night, he still wasn't too concerned, even if he thought it weird to have the same dream twice. Now, after the third time the previous night along with two other stories about dreams coming true, it became…intriguing.

His dream has him stopping by Jennifer's house. She answers the door wearing a sun dress with pockets. He asks if they can talk. She leads him to the living room where she stands near the fireplace, her back turned. He apologizes and explains that he doesn't remember that fateful night, doesn't know the girl, never saw her after that, doesn't know if anything even happened, though both of them were naked. When he finishes, she stands without speaking, hands in the dress pockets. Then…

…nothing. Each night, the dream ended with a mental jolt, like an internal thunderclap, and he bolted upright in bed, dazed, but recalling the dream in vivid detail.

Three nights. Not the week Agnes reported, but still…it had to mean something, didn't it? With the story his coworker told him and the article, it had to mean something. Didn't it?

As the caboose rumbled by and the red and white bars lifted, Bob wondered if, maybe, just maybe, like Agnes and the other dreamers, he and Jennifer could find harmony.

3

At half past five that Friday afternoon, he met Steve McArthur at Lobo's Pub. He and Steve knew each other from their university days. While Bob had gone into financial consulting, Steve chose psychiatry. They had kept in touch and every other week, met for a drink, just to catch up.

They exchanged brief reports on their jobs, Steve's latest girlfriend, Bob's mother's latest blood work.

Bob, however, soon turned the topic to which he'd been eager to discuss. "Have you heard anything about people having the same dream night after night and meeting the person they're dreaming about only find out that person also had the same dream?" Bob told him the stories his landlady and coworker had told him.

Steve nodded, sipped his martini. "Yeah, Jim Stone, one of my colleagues over in Springfield called me a few weeks ago, said he had a guy with this recurring dream. Guy came back later to say he met with the girl he dated in school who also had been having the same dream. Said they made up and are together again. Jim wanted to know what I thought of it."

"What did you tell him?"

"Said I didn't know what to think. I'd never heard of that. I guess it could happen. I'm not saying I believe in psychic connections, but there have been stories throughout the decades. You know, some woman thinks about her friend she hasn't seen in ages and that friend calls her five minutes later."

"I've heard of that, too," Bob said. "But these are dreams. The *same* dream over and over."

"Again, I don't know what to tell you. I didn't really get into dream states during my studies. I've read about dreams, of course, but not extensively."

"What do you know?"

"Just the basics." Steve took another sip. "Dreams are one way the mind sorts out the day's activities, relieves any built-up tension. They can be a way to solve problems. You know, an author writes a complex scene but doesn't have an ending. That night, he dreams the answer."

"I know what you mean." Bob finished his Bud Light. "I've had that happen a few times with my clients."

"A lot of times, the dreams mean nothing. The mind remembers something about the day, or maybe something from the recent past, and at night, the subconscious brings it up again. Could be anything. A particular food eaten, a scent in the air, a flash of color on a woman's blouse. Doesn't have to be major."

"Yeah." Bob sighed. "And you've no clue to these dreams two people are having? The same dream?"

"Nope," Steve answered. "Let me guess. You've had one."

Bob held up three fingers. "Three nights in a row."

"I'll take another stab in the dark, if you'll excuse the pun. The dream is about Jennifer."

Bob nodded.

"You really messed up with her," Steve said.

"I know."

"Tell me about the dream," Steve said.

After Bob described it, he asked, "What do you think I should do about it?"

Steve shrugged. "Well, like I said, I don't know what to make of whatever is going on with some people. Could be huge coincidence. Could be latent psychic powers cropping up. Hell, could be aliens beaming invisible rays from space as an experiment."

"Thanks." Bob smirked. "You're no help."

"Seriously, I don't know. From what you told me, maybe the best thing is to go visit Jennifer, see if she's had the same dream. Maybe you can work things out."

4

After Steve left, Bob ordered a cheeseburger and fries from the menu. While he ate, he contemplated Steve's advice. Going to see Jennifer and trying to talk to her had been gnawing at him all day. If it worked for others…

Jennifer lived in a ranch style house at the end of a cul-de-sac. The neighborhood was upper middle class, quiet, with only a few residents having children. The acreage with the house actually was located a bit beyond the semicircle of the other houses, the driveway extending fifty yards. It was where he and Jennifer were going to live after they were married. She was a successful interior decorator and ended up buying the house herself as a final "screw you" to him.

Nine o'clock. The fall season gaining steam, the sun had set long ago. He parked the car in front of the closed garage door and sat for almost fifteen minutes. What would she say? Would she even allow him inside or slam the door in his face? Had she dreamed the same scenario?

The surreal nature of it all settled over him. This was it. This was the dream being played out. How would it end? It hadn't really ended the last three nights. He'd woken up before she said anything.

Jennifer opened the door seconds after he rang the bell. She wore the same yellow and blue sundress from the dream, but she had changed in the two years since he'd last seen her. In the dream, she'd been the same beautiful woman he'd dated and loved. Standing in the doorway, her face was thinner, light brunette hair dull, and she'd lost weight. The dress practically hung from her shoulders rather than her body's curves filling out the fabric with sensuality.

"Hello, Jennifer," he said.

"Bob."

He said the words from his dream. "Could we talk?"

She nodded, allowed him inside, closed the door, then led him to the living room. He was amazed at the similarity of the real thing to the dream living room. Couch, recliner, even the fireplace and stone hearth. Like in the dream, she moved to stand in front of the fire screen, facing away from him, hands in the dress pockets.

For a moment he didn't know what to say, but, almost as if he'd memorized the script—he had, hadn't he? —he repeated the words from the dream. Telling her how stupid he'd been, that the woman was a stranger and he'd never contacted her after that night. Apologizing for his heartlessness.

When he finished, he went quiet. This was where his dream ended, where he woke up after a mental slam.

He waited. When Jennifer didn't respond, he said, "So, um, there's this weird thing going around where two people have had the same dream. I was wondering if you'd had mine. I mean, this here is *my* dream being played out."

"Yes, Bob," she said just above a whisper. "I've had the same dream." She still hadn't turned but remained facing the mantle, hands in her pockets.

Bob nodded. "Well, in my dream, this is as far as I've gotten. I apologize, then...I wake up. It's sort of a violent awakening. I don't understand it."

"I do," Jennifer said.

"Really?" Bob sighed in relief. The reconciliation was at hand.

"Yes, Bob. See, you dreamed what you were going to do and say. From your point of view. While it was the same dream, mine was from my point of view."

"Sure," Bob said. "That makes sense."

"You really hurt me two years ago, Bob. I wasn't just heartbroken. I was completely shattered. My life hasn't been the same since. I'm failing in my business. I don't have too many clients anymore. I can barely pay the bills I bother to open. I'm behind on the mortgage."

"Jennifer—"

"All because of you. I loved you so much, Bob. You were my life, my world. What you did devastated that world. I lost my way. I lost myself."

Bob had no reply, couldn't find the words.

"Then, three nights ago, I had the dream. Somehow, I knew it would come true. You'd be here, saying what you said in the dream. For me, though, I knew how the dream ended."

"How?"

Jennifer turned and gave him a sad smile. Her right hand withdrew from the pocket. She gripped a semi-automatic. She raised the gun, aimed it at his chest. "Because I end it."

5

From the AP desk:
Do dreams really come true? For some, they do, but not in the way they thought. The number of reports of simultaneous

dreams that subsequently are lived out in reality has grown in the last ten weeks. However, what started as old friends and lost relations meeting for happy reunions has turned deadly. Six murders have been associated with these "dreams come to life." Police in as many states have reported...

In related news, coffee sales have jumped nearly 200% since the last quarter...

Mayhem on the *Mercedes*
Anthony Samuels

Nigel, and his 36-year-old brother Tyler, stood waiting in their SCUBA gear in the rear of their buddy Jack's 25-foot boat, *Ladies First*. Its sonar searched the bottom for their dive destination towing behind their bright red dive flag on a 150-foot yellow float line. While they crisscrossed the ocean's floor, warm salt water splashed their faces as the waves broke against the hull. Tyler called in sick from his college teaching job where he was a biology instructor at nearby BAU to partake in this dive trip. Jack and I were freelance writers for the "Daily Sun", so we were able to set our own hours.

Today's excursion was nothing simple, a 110-foot-deep spearfishing dive without an anchor line, swimming straight into the strong currents below. Our aim was a 200-foot-long freighter named the *Mercedes* which was purposely sunk in 1985 as part of Broward County's artificial reef program. The wreck sat upright off Ft Lauderdale's Oakland Park Boulevard in a north to south orientation, next to a coral reef on its west side and a flat, barren, sandy bottom on its east. The ship achieved notoriety on nationwide TV when it ran aground in posh West Palm Beach during Hurricane Andrew next to Rose Kennedy's estate. Its bow rested in her swimming pool, and it took four months to haul the vessel away. This shipwreck was still intact and was now partly overgrown in coral and algae. The *Mercedes* was home to schools of fish such as grunts, amberjack and barracuda and large gamefish like gray grouper, red snapper and hogfish.

"The *Mercedes* should be showing up on the depth recorder soon," Jack remarked while taking a sip from his can of soda.

"Great! Tyler and I are starting to get hot in our wetsuits. We'll be about 40 minutes on the bottom, Jack. Start looking for us then."

"If we don't find any grouper or snapper on the wreck, let's swim over to the reef for lobster," my blond-haired brother Tyler suggested. He always had all the luck, catching the biggest lobster in size and the most in number of anyone. When we swam along the bottom and approached a large coral head and Tyler breaks to the left while I the right, he's the one who always found the lobster on his side while I found none on mine. The same thing applied to spearfishing. Tyler always seemed to land the biggest gamefish in size and most gamefish in number of anyone on the dive boat. No matter how hard I to tried to outdo him, my younger brother seemed to come out on top.

"Good idea," I replied feeling a little tight in my wet suit. After an enduring period of time sweltering in the sun, Jack discovered the wreck on the depth recorder screen and shouted the words we were just dying to hear: "Dive! Dive! Dive!"

My brother, spear gun and lobster bag in hand, plunged in first taking the float line with him, then myself. Two splashes, lots of bubbles, as we both disappeared below. Nothing but the dive flag floating on the surface, tethered to my brother, to mark our position. This was better known as "drift diving" to the underwater community.

There was nothing to guide our descent as the *Mercedes* was too deep to see at the onset of our dive. We both had to kick hard, swimming downward as quickly as we could to avoid being swept away from our destination by the ocean's currents. Deeper and deeper we descended into the increasingly cold and murky water below us. We left reality as we knew it above. There were no sounds except for those of compressed air being drawn from our tanks and exhaled through the regulators with each breath. The only conspicuous object to focus on was my brother swimming six feet below me. Being weightless, only our bubbles told us which direction was up.

Halfway down we were greeted by several large fish that swam up from the *Mercedes*. There were long, silver barracuda, large gray and yellow amberjack and smaller but more colorful yellow, orange and blue bottom fish. When we eventually saw and touched down on the bottom, we could not visualize the wreck anywhere. It was dark and eerie, and the clarity of the water was poor. Water at this depth filtered out much of the sunlight resulting in few and muted colors, mainly just various shades of gray. Underwater flashlights would permit more illumination and bring back those lost but vivid hues. We cocked our spear guns by drawing back on the elastic bands, snapping them into place and followed the trail of fish that swam up to meet us, realizing they will ultimately lead us to our destination.

We could not perceive what loomed directly in front of us even though it's a short distance away, ironic for a massive 200-foot-long vessel that one should have easily visualized from afar. Then, like magic, the stern appeared, veiled in mist like water, standing dead ahead. Large swarms of small reef fish and bottom fish circled above the ship which was partially covered with silt, coral, and vegetation, incompletely obscuring its name on the stern. The craft was so large it took up our entire field of vision, and from our position near the stern, we could not visualize the bow, cloaked in dusky water. That's it! The *Mercedes*. We both realized we had just ventured upon the freighter and nodded our heads to each other in applause. After a brief trek to the vessel, Tyler secured the yellow float line to the ship's stern railing jutting directly above its name. And as good fortune would have it, we soon saw vague movement in the water ahead. Advancing towards us from the bow were five undulating shadows close to the hull, swimming in formation. At first glance I assumed they were a school of large amberjack in approximately the 20-to-30-pound range. But as they approached, I could make out their details. They were our prized game fish – large, gray groupers.

Tyler and I sprang into action as we lunged towards our prey with guns thrust in front of us to aim and to give us more range. Our bodies were in the horizontal plane with our heads up, legs straight out to produce the greatest thrust with our kicks. Breathing switched from slow, deep inhalations to more rapid and shallow ones. These game fish perceived the change of habitus and broke rank, swimming away in fear. My brother was ahead of me getting the first pick of the groupers. He tracked a solitary one, the largest of the pack, that had been undecided about us from the onset and merely offered token defensive maneuvers.

Pointing his spear gun at the target, Tyler patiently waited until the fish turned more broadside so the spear tip did not skirt its flesh upon impact. Then "swoosh", that unmistakable metallic sound of the spear shaft that traveled through the gun and out the muzzle towards its destination, merely five feet away. Our guns used "free shafts" in that the spears were not connected by a string or cable. This provided for greater range and accuracy. However, you must be swift in rounding up that speared fish or otherwise you may lose not only your prey but also your expensive spring steel shaft. For this very reason my brother and I always fixed a spare to the undercarriage of our guns. We both watched as the spear struck the grouper's head in front of the gill plate and penetrated half its length. The fish writhed and contorted itself to free the spear while blood, the color green at this depth, bellowed through its gill slits.

Surprising, Tyler's perfect aim did not yield an unequivocal "kill shot". He darted forward to grasp the end of his shaft and retrieve his prey. However, the wounded fish was alive enough to evade his efforts and swam to the deck of the *Mercedes*, retreating into one of its enormous cargo holds. Tyler was not far behind. A trail of exhaled air bubbles marked his track into the darkness of the hold. I chose my grouper from the school and started making aggressive moves towards it. I hunted my fish the length of the freighter and west towards the coral reef where it eluded me in the turbid water. Damn it! It was a big one too. Swimming back to the wreck looking for Tyler in the cargo hold that he vanished into, I discovered he was not to be found. Neither were any of his bubbles visible.

Ignoring my competitive urge to continue the hunt, I deflated my vest to decrease my buoyancy and plunged into the bowels of the cargo hold in search of him. Being as dark as pitch inside, I located my flashlight attached to my weight belt and turned it on. We always stayed together when we SCUBA dive, a golden rule, in case one of us gets into trouble. Now I could not see him anywhere. My flashlight illuminated the hold as I scan the immense room. I panned the area only to discover schools of small yellow grunts and orange-colored snappers. One always feared the worst for your dive buddy when you become separated under these circumstances. Images toyed with your mind, such as an equipment malfunction or finding him struggling to free himself if his gear or wet suit became snared in the tangled mess of metal debris scattered throughout the interior. Where could he have gone? He must have followed the impaled grouper out of the vessel and down the port side into the sand covered flat. I'll search for him there. Pressing the power inflator button on my buoyancy compensator to re-inflate my vest, I turned my head upwards as I started my climb out of the cargo hold.

When I arrived at the top and grasp the railing on the walkway, I eventually saw Tyler's bubbles. They were moving up the hull from the port side. My brother was not far behind but this time he is swimming erratically, glancing all about. He was without the grouper or his spear shaft. When he drew close, I could see a contorted face of terror through his mask. His widely dilated pupils, raised eyebrows, and rapid breathing through his regulator told it all. Tyler joined me standing by the bow railing still looking around. Then he clutched my vest with his free hand and began screaming at me, but only the sound of bubbles came out of his regulator. So, he used the sign language we established for underwater communication. Tapping his thumb to the outstretched index and middle fingertips in a pincher like movement, then moving both of his hands out far from each other indicated: *shark, very large*!

We both searched side to side and up and down the wreck with no shark visible. Several brief moments passed. Finally, from the darkness below emerged a colossal figure soaring upwards toward us, omnipotent through the dimmed waters. Its immense tail fin propelled it through the murk and mist and into view. It was a gray colored tiger shark evident by the dark stripes running vertically along its flanks. The man eater glided upwards in front of the bow, mammoth like in its dimensions, a whopping 25 feet long.

The tiger shark positioned itself 100 feet away and began making concentric circles around and slightly above us constantly eyeing us both. Soon we discerned the circles were becoming closer and tighter. This tiger was considerably larger than the customary 12-to-15-foot adult size. I suspected it must have been a genetic mutation or a prehistoric throwback hidden by the ocean depths. Rows of teeth protruded from its jaws like sabers, with five or six remoras following closely behind its caudal fin.

Tyler and I positioned ourselves defensively on the deck next to the ship's wheelhouse. We were back-to-back, our spear guns cocked, not that they would do much against a creature of this size. I did not want to take my eyes off this predator but I must check the air pressure in my tank. I reached down and grasped my gauge, 1100 psi, a third of a tank of compressed air left. Tyler checked his gauge also, 950 psi. Both of us showed each other's dials as we took up our vigilant watch of our captor.

I managed not to let Tyler know this before our dive because he considered them illegal. I brought along my spring activated "power head" to use on any large game fish we happened upon that were too big for the traditional spear gun.

Luckily, I stowed it away in my vest pocket after waterproofing the bullet casing of its 0.357 magnum shell with clear fingernail polish the night before. Little did I realize I would use it to fend off a monstrous shark that had us both entrapped. Getting the cylinder-shaped, three-inch power head out of my vest pocket, I fixed it to the tip of my spear above its barb with a single wing nut. After securing it tightly in place I presented it to Tyler. Next, I pointed to the shark. By this time the only response I mustered from him was an affirmative nod and a few extra bubbles through his regulator. Several more concentric passes cut the shark's distance from us in half. I stood by for the optimal moment to mount my assault hoping the volley from the power head would stun him long enough for Tyler and me to make our mad dash for safety. Sensing the opportune moment, I tensed my muscles, coiled my body and launched, springing forward with my spear gun in front, kicking with all my strength towards the Paleolithic monster. I fired the spear gun at his head when I was six or seven feet away and waited for the tremendous underwater explosion and concussion wave it would produce.

Only it was I who is in shock as I watched the shaft leave my gun, proceed merely a few feet beyond its length and strike the shark in the head behind his eye and in front of the gill plate. I was stunned. I could not believe the power head just bounced off, failing to detonate the shell on impact, leaving behind a pale scuff mark on its thick skin. *Christ, what a time for a misfire!*

For a second or two the shaft was suspended, motionless in the water. Then it drifted downward, power headfirst, with ever increasing speed until it struck bottom. There it exploded, innocuous in a cloud of sand. The blast was incredible, sending shock waves rippling through the water, ricocheting off the metal hull of the ship, vibrating the organs in my chest. The shark and I both flinched upon its detonation and momentarily established eye contact, then we swam apart. I scrambled back to the relative safety of the freighter and pondered our next move.

This predator must have alerted others as two more tiger sharks showed up on stage and began trailing the much larger one. These two tigers were the customary adult length accompanied by several more remoras that would feast on the remaining crumbs during any feeding frenzy that would ensue. There will not even be enough of our body parts remaining for a decent Christian burial.

Back on deck next to the wheelhouse with my brother, we watched helplessly as the three sharks performed threatening advances towards us, their concentric circles become tighter and tighter. I reached down and drew up my pressure gauge. Damn! Only 500 psi of air remained, about 1/6 of a tank of compressed air, scarcely enough to make it to the surface without decompression stops. My mind shifted topside as I thought of cigar smoking Jack secure on *Ladies First*. He must be on his second or third beer by now, checking out bikini clad ladies on the beach with his high-powered binoculars, while Tyler and I mulled over our demise 110 feet below him. Jack will follow the dive flag until he realized we are way past our surfacing time. Then he would call the Marine Patrol and Coast Guard for aid to retrieve his two divers who may be lost somewhere at sea. What will Jack tell our wives if he returned to shore without us? Sherri would be crying out to Jack that I promised to protect my younger brother no matter what the circumstances may be. My wife, Lucy, would be a hysterical if she was told that they never found our bodies. And both our families' children. I glanced once more at my pressure gauge. My thought processes were now being overwhelmed by fear concerning our remaining air, only 300 psi now remained. That was it. We had to take our chances and make a frantic swim for Jack's boat. Perhaps one of us would come back alive to tell our tale. Pointing my pressure gauge at my brother's facemask, I motioned upwards with my index finger of my other hand. My brother glimpsed at his air pressure gauge, then looked back at me with eyes wide open. He nodded in the affirmative.

As our muscles tensed in order to spring off the deck, Tyler and I stared at each other with question marks in both our eyes.

Amazed, we both heard the same metallic clanging sounds accompanied by several more in rapid succession. They appeared to be arising from behind us, some place deep in the wheelhouse. Next, a dark image scampered though an open wheelhouse window. It was the grouper that Tyler had previously shot, swimming as fast as it could. The spear shaft was still jutting out from its flank causing the fish to swim awkwardly, listing to one side, with a faint trail of blood streaming behind it. After being speared, the wounded grouper must have sought refuge and holed up in the recesses of the wheelhouse. Like us, anticipating its impending doom, he made a break for it eastward, towards the more open and deeper waters, out of the bounds of the vessel where we all would certainly be entombed. Struggling to free itself from the close quarters of the wheelhouse and swim through the open window, it must have struck the shaft against the steel hull producing the metallic sounds we heard.

We both observed as the school of encircling sharks broke rank and raced towards the impaled grouper, with the big tiger leading the way. It merely took a few seconds for the tiger shark to catch up to and completely engulf his prey in its massive jaws. Green colored blood spurted out from the predator's mouth and gill slits and was seemingly everywhere. The tiger thrashed his head back and forth and devoured the fish whole, spitting out the spear shaft like a toothpick at a cocktail party. We next saw the entire entourage swim into the deeper, darker waters until they all disappeared out of sight, as if nothing ever happened.

Tyler and I glanced at each other shrugging our shoulders, refusing to believe what we had just witnessed. We hand signaled our remaining air supply with two fingers, 200 psi remaining each. I just hoped we had enough air remaining to make it to the surface.

The Ritual

Davros Jovanka

I believe God rejoices in His triumphs, but I also believe His opposite celebrates victories just as joyously. I have seen evil in my life, but what I have witnessed in the past hours has been beyond even my vast imagination. I didn't realize what was happening until after facts revealed themselves. The supposed coincidences and deceptions were so clever, I had no inkling how everything was so wrong. I was blind, as many others were. However, if I have enough time to record my experiences maybe, if anyone finds these pages, the next man may be warned.

*　*　*

We were lost. If we hadn't been having so much fun, I wouldn't blamed Lorraine. It was her suggestion to take the long way home— "the scenic route" she called it. Back roads took us through lush wooded areas, alongside clear gurgling streams, past dilapidated yet aesthetically beautiful farm buildings. On several occasions, we stopped and smelled the sweet air and let our eyes take in nature at its finest. However, while my senses reveled, I forgot the way home. Even making a U-turn away from the setting son only seemed to put us deeper into the maze of narrow roads that were more like trails. I didn't recognize any landmarks. Across open fields or meadows, no lights shone from farmhouses.

Part of me couldn't complain too much. The Saturday had been one of the few Lorraine and I managed to spend together. Her job kept taking her away nearly every weekend. I had been understanding at first but as the months passed, those weekend days alone became more difficult to tolerate alone. Besides, it was our first wedding anniversary.

I used to live in Milford, Pennsylvania, employed as a literary agent for a New York City company. Normally, I made the two-hour trip to the home office about once every two weeks. One day, during lunch at a local bistro, someone bumped the back of my chair. "Excuse me," she said. When she stepped into view...well, that was the beginning of my downfall. High cheeks, full lips, dark, violet eyes, a mass of hair ink black yet the sun caught sparkles of dark orchid purple and sangria. Around thirty but with a presence of ageless maturity that gave her a majestic air.

She had thought there was an empty table on the crowded restaurant patio and was making her way back inside. On impulse, I invited her to sit with me.

Lorraine worked as a realtor in Pittsfield, Massachusetts. She had come to the city for a vacation.

We talked, exchanged numbers, and the relationship began. Two and half hours away from each other, but we took turns driving the distance or meeting in the middle to see each other. Almost a year later, we were married.

She convinced me to move to a small town in western Massachusetts where she quickly gained a respectable and lucrative position with a local realtor firm. I still enjoyed the quiet, the fresh air, and the serenity. For her, however, the new locale brought a drastic change to her schedule. Five days in the office and most weekends on the road.

At first, I wondered if this weekend was going to be any different. Despite our anniversary, I half expected her to pack up the usual overnight bag for another business jaunt. She surprised me when she said she had been looking forward to our one-year celebration. I thought she'd be expecting an expensive dinner, but she suggested, quite sincerely, to a quiet day in the country even farther away from our little burg. I'd wear my pressed suit on another occasion. I switched plans to present her with an anniversary diamond over tuna salad and Dr Pepper instead of prime rib and Chablis.

Up until dusk, it was complete bliss. We drove northwest and somewhere near the New Hampshire border, we stopped by a little stream and lunched in the shade of a lush hemlock tree. The day was warm with a slight breeze that tempered the sun's heat.

We walked, laughed, and ate. I presented the jewel on top of a chocolate chip cookie. Reviving our honeymoon days, we made love under the tree.

To wind down, we traveled the countryside, discovering quaint farms, rolling meadows, and as I mentioned before, taking

Lorraine's suggestions and getting more off the beaten track. The landscape soon lost identification. One road blended into another. Some ended without warning and others faded to cart tracks. Most stretched for miles without end. I would have stopped to ask directions, but the collapsed farmhouses hadn't seen human life in decades.

Night advanced upon us and the roads became more indistinguishable, the air hazy with the day's heat. I couldn't tell if I'd been over certain stretches of road, going in circles. With nothing else, I followed Lorraine's decisions even though we weren't seeing any signs of life, certainly no lights of even small villages.

Pavement ended and gravel and dirt took over. Darkness crowded the headlights, and I missed seeing a deep rut. The car jolted to a stop. Lorraine and I weren't injured, just shaken. Grabbing the flashlight, I kept under the seat, we exited the automobile. The light revealed a flat tire and a bent wheel. I sank to the ground in despair. Lorraine came to me, knelt, hugged me, and assured me that everything would be all right. I smiled and told her I loved her.

The star-filled sky held no moon. The woods were so thick, the light barely penetrated the first line of trees.

"Any suggestions now?" I meant it as a half joke as I'd been followed her directions, but her face tightened. I adjusted my tone to apology. "Sorry. I'm not blaming you." Maybe I was, though.

"If we start going east, we'll hit the ocean sooner or later," she said.

It wasn't a bad idea. Not that we'd reach the Atlantic, but it was our best chance of stumbling across a major highway and, it happened to be the direction the car faced.

Lorraine retrieved a plastic water bottle she'd brought from the back seat and we set off. We'd gone perhaps a mile when a solitary dot of light shone from perhaps another quarter mile away. The road ended at a small dirt walkway that led to a stone building with a pitched roof. Maybe a caretaker's house with a larger estate farther on or maybe even an old church. The building sat at an angle to the walkway so the wooden front door lay in shadows. The light shone through one of the side windows. Weeds and ivy hugged the walls.

Lorraine and I drew near the window as if we shared a curiosity to peer inside before knocking on the door. Yes, it was a church, but nothing remotely like Baptist or Lutheran church. In fact, it was quite the opposite of any Christian denomination. Poe or Lovecraft might have written about such a place.

The "sanctuary" was a mixture of reds, blacks, and purples. These were primarily expressed through the cloaks at least a dozen figures wore as they surrounded a sacrificial altar in the center of the room. Tapestries of assorted sizes adorned with unknown alien symbols hung on the walls. More symbols had been etched into the stones on the walls that could be seen. The stones themselves were dark and sinister as if take from an elaborate system of catacombs. The floor was laid out in a circular pattern spiraling in toward the altar.

The altar itself was a chunk of granite with sat upon a stone platform. A perimeter trough angled to the foot of the table, and into a spout that went into the floor. Black candles flickered at each corner. They illuminated the victim whose wrists and ankles were secured to wooden stakes embedded into the stone. Naked, he strained against his bonds, screaming entreaties.

The group encircling the altar all wore cloaks of reds and purples with more of those fantastical symbols woven into the fabric. Hoods partially concealed their faces, but the countenances I did make out in additional to longer hair strands poking from the hoods told me they were all women. Youthful women, all around the same age as my wife. Stunningly gorgeous faces that could grace fashion magazine covers.

As the group moved in a languid pace around the altar, their arms created shapes in the air and a low murmuring emanated from their unmoving lips. Their unrecognizable words came through the windows as almost as a vibration.

One woman, perhaps the leader, wore a half mask and carried a knife with a double-sided blade that must have been at least seven inches long. She stood broadside to the victim and passed the knife over his body in rhythm with the murmurings that my recognized as more of a chant than random foreign words. Eyes closed; her body swayed with the motion of her arms.

I gripped Lorraine's arm but neither of us looked away from the scene. The knife-wielding woman swayed faster. The others' movements intensified, the chant rising in volume and pitch. At the crescendo, the knife was poised high above the man, tip aiming at his navel. His eyes dilated. Muscles and veins tightened the skin as he strained against the binds. His screams filled the air when the blade descended and impaled his lower abdomen then became inhuman when the woman wrenched the weapon toward his sternum. Blood gurgled from the ma's mouth. Removing the blade, the woman inserted her hand into the bloody wound. Her arm tensed, gave a slight tug, and withdrew. The man's screaming cut off and his body dropped, lifeless to the stone as blood flowed from the wound and dripped from the woman's arm.

She held up her hand to present the still pulsing, muscular object in her crimson-soaked fist. The other participants in this abominable scene drifted toward the leader as she stepped from the altar platform. The gathered around her as she held the heart high, then let it fall to the floor. Before it hit the stones, the women scrambled forward, squealing and growling like crazed cats, each trying to get a piece to consume.

The moment froze. The still warm corpse of the man. Blood flowing into the spout and down into the floor. The head woman standing in all her demonic glory, blood-streaked arms spread as if in exuberant praise. The others with mouths of scarlet.

I whirled away from the window, sickened. The vileness of the scene forced me to my knees, retching.

"Drink this." Lorraine offered the water bottle. "It'll help."

I grabbed the bottle, flipped up the cover, upended the bottle, and gulped down the entire contents. Finished, I leaned against the stone wall, breaths coming deep and labored. "What the hell was that?" I said.

"Not hell, my darling," Lorraine said. "Irkatta's followers enjoy heaven and long-lasting life."

Her words drifted into my ears as through a pool of water. My head swam under the surface of that pool. What was she saying? What was going…

I awoke to more horror as I had become a part of it. Upon opening my eyes, I viewed the room not from outside the window...but from the angle of the man on the table. I had replaced that hapless soul upon that stone altar. Hands and ankles tethered with unyielding leather straps to the wooden pegs. The granite cooled my skin and sent chills through my naked body.

I tried to see as much of the room as possible. Everywhere, from the wooden rafters to the walls to the tapestries those drawn symbols dominated. Weird and foreign, otherworldly, nothing recognizable to anything in history books or from any culture I'd ever studied. As my eyes took it all in, each drawing or carving seemed to coalesce into one large, interconnected picture, each in grotesque juxtaposition to the next, each a part of a larger whole. The illusion or rather, the reality appeared. Those on the walls correlated with those sewn into the tapestries. Like stars on a planetarium's dome, they formed a gigantic constellation, disappearing if focused up on to intently. The formation that metamorphosed seemed almost tangible, sentient...watching. Watching me.

A voice broke through my mind's reeling, my reason trying to figure out this nightmare, my panic wanting escape. A woman stood at a doorway, staring at me. She was dressed in the cloak and hood of the others I'd seen but instantly recognizable. Lorraine.

"Lorraine," I called. "What's going on. Get me out of here?"

She walked to the altar, stepped up to the platform and looked down at me. Her face was serene, a slight smile upon her lips.

"I hope you will feel honored, John. You should. Not many men get to experience the Sharing. Some don't make it that far. Some die of fright before the ceremony even begins, and then he is no longer useful. The heart has to be beating when it is extracted of the...essence disappears too quickly to be of value." She ran her fingers over the edge of the grooved altar. "I hoped I hadn't given you too much of the sedative. It would have been disappointing for you not to share in the ecstasy.

As I write these memories, I shudder at the words she used. *The ecstasy.*

I had strained and pulled against the bonds. "What the hell are you talking about? Lorraine, what is this?"

"Oh, John, I apologize. I got ahead of myself." She walked to the foot of the altar, and stood, legs apart, over the spout and channel that ran into the stone floor. "I should explain. Back before the earth became form and void, Lucifer and his minion's rejected heaven. One of those was named Irkatta, and she became one with the earth, offering extended life for those who worshiped her and offered sacrifices. Even after the great flood, she still existed. As the population grew, she attracted more followers. While some sects were wiped out, others continued, moving from country to country and across the oceans."

I could only stare, mind reeling with this absurd, impossible tale.

"The members are all female, of course, akin to mother earth, akin to Irkatta who gives life. We're free to marry and have children, but continual sacrifices must be made, usually on the first anniversary of the wedding."

She ran her fingers up my leg as she moved toward my head. I shivered at her touch, remembered the pleasures it so often brought me. She leaned over my face. "John, I'm over 300 years old, have been married scores of times with as many children. In fact, I'm pregnant now. The little girl inside me will be so blessed and will eventually join Irkatta's ranks."

She moved to my head and I had an upside-down view of her. "Final preparations are being made, John. You will share with us your essence, your heart, and your blood. Irkatta drinks twice tonight and will be pleased. Each of us will share and be blessed with life."

She left the room, leaving me reviled at her words, at this entire nightmare. I struggled with the bonds again but to no avail.

How could Lorraine be part of this hellish cult? Irkatta? Extended life through sacrifices? It was unreal, yet...

The past year. Our life together. A sham? A setup to...this? Had there been any real love or just waiting? All of those weekends away. Where had she gone? Here for other sacrifices?

Bile rose to burn my throat. No, it couldn't be true.

Extended life. Delayed aging. What about health? Lorraine had never been sick. No allergies, no minor colds. Even her monthly periods came and went with no apparent change in mood or behavior.

This weekend. This day. The picnic...her idea. The location...her idea. The 'innocent' suggestions to turn here, take that road there after we became lost. She hadn't been lost. She knew exactly where we were going. The rut. Was it planned?

Had every detail of our marriage been arranged for this night? My presence on the altar was the answer.

A column of cloaked and hooded women filing into the room interrupted my thoughts. The ceremony I'd witness through the window was about to begin, but I was the man to be cut open. It was my heart to be removed and consumed by these women.

They encircled the alter and the leader stepped forward. She stepped up and gazed at each woman in turn, as if to assure herself everyone was present.

"To the world, Irkatta is all!" she said.

The others echoed the words.

"Irkatta is the world."

Again, the repeated reply.

"Life is because of Irkatta."

"Irkatta is life," the women replied.

They began their circling of the altar murmuring undecipherable words, arms in front creating the weird angled shapes in the air. The leader produced the blade, silver gleaming in the candlelight. Flames reflected from the blade with each pass over my body.

I didn't scream but fought all the more against the leather straps. I bucked and tried to kick, contorted my body for any opening.

At one point, the leader stopped her movements and the women halted to face the altar. "Who claims this male?" she said.

"I do, mistress," Lorraine said.

This was part of the ceremony we must have missed. We had come upon the scene mid-ritual.

"Join me," the head woman said.

Lorraine stepped from the circle to stand beside the woman.

"Have you fulfilled all of the requirements for the Sharing?"

"I have, mistress," Lorraine answered.

"Are you willing to give this male to Irkatta so that She may give us life?"

"I am, mistress."

"May it be so."

The leader handed the knife to Lorraine and took the empty space in the circle. I remembered the last victim. Had he been *her* husband? Was the wife required to kill her own mate?

Again, the women murmured the alien words while encircling the altar. Lorraine swayed to the motion and cut shapes in the air.

"Lorraine! Stop this madness." My entreaty went ignored. There was no stopping this.

Instead of screaming or begging, I renewed my effort to free myself. Sweat coated my skin and a tangy and fetid odor filled the air. It could have been my own fear seeping from my pores. Mouth dry, I wrenched my arms...

...and something loosened. My eyes went to the strap around my right wrist. A notch in the band had stretched. If I was patient—slow movements—I might work my hand out of the loop. I twisted and pulled, relaxed and tugged. The ridge of my knuckles wouldn't slide free. I compressed my hand and eased it toward my head. Slowed my breathing to relax more.

The ceremony neared the fateful moment, the volume of the chants rose. Lorraine grasped the knife, raised it above my stomach.

I inhaled, held my breath, twisted my hand...and the knuckles slid free.

The knife descended. I wrenched my body away as far as the other straps allowed. The point of the blade struck the stone table. Shock of the impact threw Lorraine off balance. I took advantage of the moment, whirled back, and slammed my elbow into her face. She dropped the knife and stumbled back off the platform.

Fingers found the knife and I stretched to cut the leather of my other wrist.

The other women had come out of whatever trance they were in and all gazed at Lorraine crying out in pain, blood flowing from her nose.

I sat up and with two quick slices, cut the ankles straps.

The women reached for me. I stood and leaped over their heads. Landing hard on the stone floor, I bent my knees, rolled, came up, and ran for the opening I thought the women had come through.

Stone wall. No doorway. Where was it? No time. Only one choice remained.

I turned, tensed, and plowed through the grasping hands and raking claws of nails. Back up to the platform, I leaped off the altar toward the window. Three steps and I dove through. Glass scraped my skin like I'd slid through a circled of nails.

I landed hard on the ground, forced away the pain, scrambled to my feet, and dashed away.

Behind me the women shrieked. Above their wailing the mistress called, "Catch him! Irkatta must not be denied!"

The ground shivered in a tremor as if a sonic boom had gone off under the forest floor. I echoed back and forth.

"Irkatta calls us!" the mistress yelled. "She demands blood!"

I didn't look back but found the dirt road and took off. Embedded glass pricked my skin with each footfall and blood streaked my body, but I kept running.

*   *   *

The road on which I had fled crossed a stream. Instead of continuing, I diverted off the road to follow the contours of the water. I lost track of time. Twenty minutes or hours later, I reached a clearing with a weather-beaten shack that titled with age and deterioration. I searched the gloomy interior and found a table, with a dusty candle. On a counter my hand touched a box of matches. The small sticks were moist to the touch, but it may have been the blood on my fingers. Three of the matches disintegrated before one flared to life. The wick hungrily accepted the flame.

Further exploration resulted in yellowing sheets of paper and a stub of a pencil which I now use to write this story.

Exhaustion, terror, and heartbreak war for dominance. Oh, Lorraine. I have loved you as no other in my life. What betrayal you have given me. I've been but a pawn in some ancient way of life. A religion kept alive by blood of men.

I still can't quite accept this. Were those women all centuries old? Perhaps...millennia?

What about the shock wave when I escaped? Irkatta? A living deity under the earth? Part of the earth? One that consumed the blood of slaughtered victims? How many other sects of this cult existed around the world?

Wait! Sounds from without. Rustling in the nearby woods. Twigs and stick snapping. An animal?

Can I last until morning? Will I be able to find my way to civilization? All I'd need would be a telephone poll, a distant water tower, a cow in a field to evidence people nearby.

More sounds. No, low voices. Growls that sound inhuman, yet I know they derive from the throats of Irkatta's women. I have been discovered. I'm too exhausted to run.

But my story is finished. I will secret these pages under a floorboard and hope that someone will find them, read my words, believe them, then hunt down this cult wherever it may exist, and wipe out every member. Maybe then, the being—if it is truly a creature from eons past—will also die.

They're coming for me. They know I am here. Flashlight beams lance the darkness from the trees. Snarling and howling madness from the woods.

Minutes left, I wonder what will become of my body, my soul. Will they sacrifice me here or drag me back to that accursed church of horror? Maybe I'll succumb to insanity and be spared the agony.

Faces emerge now from the trees. No longer angelic, but mutated, alien, ugly. Are these their true selves?

They are at the door. I finish and hide these papers. Please, I pray that someone finds—

*   *   *

VERMONT STATE POLICE CRIME REPORT

Two hikers (names listed below) discovered handwritten pages in an old cabin near the head of an unnamed stream half a mile east of Blue Trail. Investigators found no blood or evidence of any crime at the cabin or the surrounding clearing and woods.

Further investigation into the alleged incident described in the pages resulted in no conclusive evidence any real crime took place. No "church" or similar type building was found within a twenty-mile radius. Massachusetts has no records of any resident of Pittsfield or neighboring towns by the name of Lorraine. No records were found of any property purchased or owned by anyone named John or Lorraine in the whole of the state. Further investigations into New York City literary agencies turned up no employee named John who lived in Milford, Pennsylvania.

The case was officially closed with the determination that the story, the characters, and the crimes of sacrificial murder, to be fictional. It is not known why the author hid the pages beneath the cabin's floor.

*   *   *

Eighteen months later

Dave,

I hope you and Susan don't stay out too late tonight (lol), but I don't think our cat will mind a late-night visit. It does enjoy when you visit. I left the key in the usual spot.

I'm really happy my wife convinced me to move to West Virginia. I never thought I'd like small-town life, but you and Susan have made it so easy to make friends. I was amazed you two were married the same day as Lorraine and I. Happy one-year anniversary.

Not sure when we'll be back. Lorraine planned a great day exploring the back roads. A picnic, maybe some hiking.

Catch you soon.

Franklin

Dracovich Manor
Michael Van Natta

I thought I knew West Followell's End pretty well, having lived here all my life, that life so far being nineteen and a half years. Never had I known such a road existed. I had to check the map. Hopeful, I'd left this delivery for last and by then, the day had taken a big ass turn for the worse.

The butt-end of October can be a bit brisk in northeast Iowa. That morning had dawned bright and sunny. I'd checked online before I left my apartment: The Dubuque Telegraph Herald called for cold and maybe some rain. Before she died, before it went online, my mother was editor of that newspaper.

By noon, the depot had put out warnings on my screen: a front was coming in.

The frigid wind whipped out of the north and down the hilly Leach Lane where I'd finally parked the brown beast. Hurrying up a broken stone path likely as not to twist or break an ankle, the wind and now drizzle came straight at my face.

I hadn't dressed warm enough. No gloves, no hat. Forgetting shit is what happens –one of the things – when I forget to take my Adderall. Still, I hadn't planned on doing that much walking. A weathered sign by the path rimmed in gold paint stood crooked: "Dracovich Manor."

With the wind and rain and all, I took it slow up the steep and overgrown twisty path. I about chewed off the ugly worry wart on my right hand. Worry: another thing. Adderall helps.

Plus, something was big time wrong with the box itself. It stunk. On the narrow road up, I noticed a bad smell that seemed to coat the inner walls of the truck. My first thought was maybe sour milk or limburger cheese left over from Harshel Beamer – the day delivery dude with oddball appetites. When I lifted the package, there was about a dozen flies swirling and landing all over it.

I managed not to fall carrying the package at arm's length and, blowing out quick clouds of frosty air, got up to the reasonable safety of the flat stones on the front stoop. I looked for a doorbell. None. Only an old-fashioned brass knocker that I realized after looking close was - not a lion's head or a deer head like you sometimes see – but a rat's head. A fucking rat's head! Beady eyes and all. Coated with a frosting of rime. Jesus.

My mother brought me up strict, taught me to be a girl of manners, routines. I don't cuss as a rule. Not out loud anyway, and never in public. Only to myself, a habit I hate but can't seem to avoid. Thinking *Fuck that* hasn't seemed to help. We all have this person we show to others, don't we? The one we want to be? The one we tell ourselves we should be more like?

I put the malodorous box down. Looking up at the front of the decrepit mansion, windows were all cracked. One of the huge stone window ledges - the one off to the right on the second floor - had broken off and sure enough, a pile of ancient masonry lay like tombstones amid the waist-high thicket of ice-coated weeds that had invaded the landscape. I gave the rat's head several swift but hard raps.

Sounds, muffled and quick, from inside. Then a crash, a shout, from just above. I took another step back and looked up in time to see a light flicker on, and then off right away though the high window without the ledge. The cold evening was whistling quiet until I heard faint music from within, a tinkling sound I recognized as Fleur-de-Les from third grade piano lessons.

Snow now. It had blown into the cracks on the fieldstone. Let's get this done. The tinkling piano ceased. I rapped the rat again and before I could take my hand off the knocker, the door pulled open and a real honest to God fucking Karen herself peeked out. I mean, white blouse buttoned all the way up, Fifties-style blonde bouffant with a blue head scarf, paisley full length swishy dress, blue eyes to match. I mean, she was perfect.

"Yes?" she said, pretty as a meadowlark. "Can I help you?"

I pointed down. "Package."

"Well, thank you, dear. Just leave it there where it is." She must have seen the flies.

"Love to, lady," I said, brushing the snowflakes from my eyelashes. "But I gotta have a signature." I looked at my device. "It's for a Frederick Dracovich. Is he here?'

The woman smiled like she was selling toothpaste on a commercial. "He is, but...I'm afraid he is in the middle of something at the moment and can't be disturbed. Are you sure you can't just leave it?"

"No. Nope, sorry. Gotta have his signature."

"Well, please come in then. I'll see what we can do."

Inside, she walked to a side table in what I envisioned a parlor would look like if I ever would see one. Hanging from the ceiling was a chandelier of crystals and real tongues of fire encased in globes of glass, giving the room a feel of being lit only in the very center – the edges faded into a gloomy darkness. Old paintings – I say old because whoever has real framed paintings? – hung on every wall.

"Put in over there," she said, indicating an umbrella stand. "I'll see if I can interrupt Frederick." She turned to an old-fashioned telephone sitting on the side table and punched a single button. It was then that I noticed she wasn't perfect at all.

Across the back of her neck and running all the way down into her collar was a ridge of protruding flesh, giving me the notion of a crested bird. It must have extended down because under her blouse, she was hump-backed. I looked away as my mother always instructed me to do when confronted with people less fortunate. It was a thing in our family because Lydia, younger than me by ten years, had these funny lips.

I made a poker face, waited while the woman talked to someone. The wind was screeching though the ancient windows making the whole house feel forlorn.

The woman set the phone down. "He can't leave what he's doing. It's very important, you know. Are you sure you can't just leave it? I could pay you to come back and get his signature tomorrow or another day?" She held out her hand and in it was a small bright chunk of something. It looked like a ring – a half ring really, broken. "It's worth about fifty dollars," she said.

I've seen some wild shit in my day but I've never seen anything like that. It looked like gold. What the hell?

She reached out her hand to mine and in a strangely intimate gesture, lifted it and opened my fist. She placed the gold thing in it and closed my fingers around it. "Dr. Dracovich would be very appreciative. He is a most generous man."

The snow was coming down in wind-blown buckets when I trudged back down the path. In only my sneakers, my toes were icicles. Must have been 5 inches on the ground in that short time. Fuck this.

When I got to the road, my truck wasn't there. My feet were freezing, my fingers numb, and the fucking truck had taken off.

By the time I made it back up to the rat's head and knocked, the meager day threatened to give up the ghost. Over a foot of snow had accumulated. I'd learned in training about the trucks and their built-in fail-safes but thought it was all made up, fucking urban legend.

"My lord, girl," the same woman gasped. "Come in, come in. You must be frozen. Let's get you warmed up."

I stomped my wet feet on a rug that resembling a thick deer skin. I had no feeling in them. She led the way to the left through double pocket doors into a dimly lit great room and sat me by a roaring fire. Two old but well-kept sofas and two chairs had been positioned beside floor lamps flickering with what looked like candlelight. Another chandelier, bigger than the one in the entryway, glowed with a dozen crystalline bulbs. A half dozen gold-framed paintings, from medieval-looking scenes to modern abstract stuff, decorated every dark paneled wall. The crackling fire drew me. I'd never been so grateful for heat.

"I'll get you some tea," the woman said after I explained how the freight company has self-driving trucks that head for home when a threat is detected. She lifted a quilt and spread it over my legs. "It'd be best to get those wet shoes off." She smiled and then hurried out.

The house itself, save the popping and sizzling of burning logs was deathly quiet. Soon, faint tinkling of glassware and then later, a whistle of a teapot came from another distant room.

Despite the comfort and the warmth, I pushed the heavy chair back away from the hearth. I fucking hate fire. It scares the hell out of me.

The heavy doors slid apart and the woman came in with a gilded tray, set it down and took the seat next to me. "There's some scones here if you're hungry," she said.

I sipped. The steaming liquid slipped down my gullet like magic.

"I'm Doris Reichert," she said. "I'm Doctor's go-to. You know…" *She looked about with wistful eyes. "Whatever he needs. Kind of like a chief of staff. What shall I call you?"

What gives with the formalities? I felt like I'd been dragged into a fucking Hansel and Gretel story like I used to read to Lydia. Still, I tried to smile. "I'm Crystal Bennington."

"You'll of course stay with us tonight, Ms. Bennington. Until the storm blows over." She left both scones on the end table. Despite my feet, which were burning from within now, hunger swept through me like an ill wind. I devoured the first in three big bites and sat back, pulled the comforter around my shoulders.

Under the crispy sound of the fire, I noticed a low droning sound from above, as if some off-balance motor moved levers, turned wheels and gears and pulleys. Yet, with the exception of the old telephone, I hadn't seen any signs that the house had any sort of electric service. I looked along the walls below the wainscoting and saw no outlets. How…? What the…? No sooner did I think that than a tinkling of piano keys caught my ear. The same song. From the next room, or somewhere close. Fluer de Lis.

The doors remained closed. Carefully, I stood, as if on pillars of wood, the toes of my feet afire with errant nerve signals – pain and heat. I walked to the corner of the room, dragging the comforter with me. Under the shade of another pole lamp, a globe of frosted glass enshrouded an actual tongue of fire. A tiny winged knob connected to the stem and with the caution I usually approach anything with flame, I turned it and saw the flicker lower and extinguish.

Gas lights? You gotta be fucking kidding.

An unmistakable odor of wax or grease surrounded the darkened lamp. Not gas then. Oil? What kind of place is this? Two doors punctuated the wall. Bedrooms? Kitchen? I tried them. Locked.

On the small antiquated table, now in shadows, sat a thick book. Leaning down to see better, the cover read in gold embossed letters: "Helmlik House" and in smaller letters below: "From Conception, Construction, and Through the Years." A picture -

what looked like a woodcut - had been impressed in the leather, *unmistakably the house in which I now sat contemplating losing my damn toes to frostbite. I couldn't help but see in my mind's eye the sign by the path. Dracovich Manor.

Huh.

Before I could look inside, the doors slid open. "Whatever are you doing, Ms. Bennington?" she said. She strode through the room, her dress swishing, and grabbed the book from my hand. Her smile returned then. She clasped the heavy tome to her chest.

"I…That's a book about this house, isn't it?"

"Let's just get you upstairs to bed now. We can look at it tomorrow before you leave, if you want."

It was the oddest fucking thing.

She led the way out to the foyer and up the grand stairs, between rows of small lamps giving off only a gloom of light. Oil lamps again?

"Unfortunately," she said as we turned on the second-floor landing and headed again up, "We had a guest last night in the Library Bedroom who left late. Just before you came, in fact." She turned away leaving me to stare at her deformed back. I thought I heard her say, in a voice that hissed a reptilian note: "Ungrateful bastard." But then louder, leading the way, "We haven't had time to prepare it for another guest. I'm afraid you have to settle for the Collections Bedroom. Come along. It's on the top floor."

By the time we set foot on the off-kilter floorboards of the third floor - a narrow hallway at best - I had slowed to a bare crawl. A tiny window at the end of the hall looked out over a thick forest.

Four openings lined the hall. On the left was a tall but narrow door adorned with small, framed panels, rail and stile.

The Collections Bedroom room was already lit with those sconces along each wall. A flood of color met my eyes. Flowers were everywhere. Vases full of yellow daffodils and blue iris, white lilies. There was even an arms-length spread over the headboard of the four poster against the back wall. Yet the air was thick, cloying, with an imposing sour smell. And cigar.

Then I saw the faces, the smirks, grimaces, the doleful agony. The heads of animals. On all the walls. A lion by a window, its golden mane matted brown. The imposing black moose on the opposite wall.

Looking around among the menagerie, three closed doors, leading where?

Doris turned. "There is a bathroom through that door." She pointed to the corner door. "There are towels, a toothbrush, soap, whatever you might need." A look of perplexity that I mistook for anger flits over her eyes and in a blink, is gone. "I think a hot bath would do you good, dear." She breezed past me and stopped at the door. "There is a bell by the bed. Ring if you need anything. Mr. King, out manservant, is quiet the insomniac."

With that, she was gone, pulling the door closed with a bang, leaving me standing in the middle. After her footsteps faded, I made it to entry door, found the lock knob and twisted it. I felt my throbbing bare feet on softness and looked to see an orange and black tiger rug.

*   *   *

There were many more faces. Small animals- a marmoset, several common squirrels, a bobcat. Stuffed heads of white mice act as a waistcoat around the room. Behind, flanking one of the doors, was a golden retriever with its tongue hanging out and a pleading Brittany spaniel, frozen in death.*** not in original story.

A heavy leather recliner sat in one corner, flanked by a side table. An ashtray there next to a glass with ice and a clear brown liquid. Wafts of smoke drifted up from a lit cigar, slowly extinguishing itself for lack of a smoker.

A bath sounded just like what the fucking doctor ordered. Maybe it was the power of suggestion. I went into the bathroom that turned out to be a throwback to some sanitarium. I turned on the faucets but before I stripped off my damp clothes, I remembered the cigar and went back, stubbed it out in the ashtray. Then, I eased my way in. I gotta tell you, nothing ever felt so good.

From somewhere deep in the house came again the tinkling piano chimes of Fleur-de-Les.

*   *   *

I woke from a swirling nightmare. Outside, a snare drum of icy snow still beat against the single window. I left my feet bare – I couldn't stand the pain of the socks, not to mention still wet shoes.

It was early Saturday morning, best guess. None of the lamps were lit. Then I remembered I'd turned them all off before I went to bed. Of course I did.

I could walk but barely. I hobbled over to one of the other doors. Locked. Tried the second one. Also locked. I limped to the hallway door that I'd locked the night before and noticed on my way that the ashtray that had held the stubbed-out cigar had been emptied and cleaned. The room was warm but a shiver ran through my veins then. I looked at the two locked doors, then tried the hall door. It, too, was locked. Once again, there was a chugging motor sound from somewhere deep within the house. An old-time radiator I hadn't seen the night before clanked against the window wall. A smell of mold drifted in the air.

I turned the small inner knob to unlock the door and then opened it.

Well, no, I didn't open it. It was locked. From the fucking outside! Without a thought, I pounded on the door with my fists. "Get me out of here!" I yelled again and again. And again, until I gave up.

I was tottering toward the bathroom when Doris fucking Day pushed through and swirled into the room. Once again, she wore a wide floor-length skirt, this time red, looking like goddam Scarlet herself.

"What the hell? You locked the fu…you locked the door, locked me in? What kind of crazy place is this? All these animal corpses? The oil lamps? And what? No electricity? What the hell is going on?"

"Please sit, Ms. Bennington," she said and pointed to a small ice cream table and chair under the frosted window. "Let's get a good look at those feet."

"Not until you tell me what's going on here. Why was I locked in?"

"Doctor insists. We've had sleepwalkers in the past. Some have injured themselves."

"But you have no right."

"Oh," she said. Her voice twisted into a snarl. "We have every right. Now sit. Please."

Fury is the best word to describe it. I felt about to erupt. "Bathroom?" I said, pointing and then without waiting for her permission, lurched through the door then banged it closed.

Sitting on the pot, I noticed a brown ring around the bathtub. Was I that dirty? I felt my cheeks flush up and reached for a towel. I started wiping off the scum, only to see it come away with glittering yellow flecks. Jesus, is that gold? No, couldn't be. Could it?

I carried the towel out and held it in front of me. "What is this stuff, Doris? It was covering the bathtub."

Something happened then with her right eye. Some sort of twitch. Her lid pulled down, held and then released. She didn't seem to notice.

"It's no secret, Ms. Bennington," she said, taking the towel from me. "It's residue from the water pipes. Happens all the time. We're used to it. I should have warned you."

"Is…is it gold? Those flakes? It looks like gold. But that can't be."

"It is gold," Doris said. "Listen. I will tell you about it. It is a fascinating story. But first, the cook, Mr. King, will bring you breakfast here in the room and then we'll get those feet fixed up. If we don't care for them properly, they'll get infected. You could lose your feet. Doctor has told me exactly what to do."

She stood and without looking back, left the room. The last I saw of her was her hunched back. She left the door open.

I sat at the ice cream table. Wind howled up and down the scale driving the snow before it. Little drifts formed over the window ledge.

Breakfast arrived, conveyed by a man no taller than my ribcage. Dressed in a white apron, he addressed me in a shrill high voice. His disposition was all bubbly-like, but his chin was outsized, and half of his forehead protruded like an orange. When he turned his head, his left ear was huge and floppy. I couldn't help but think of that Elephant Man movie. Yet he seemed unaware of his hideous looks, setting my tray on the table.

"Eggs Benidict," he chimed. "The House Special." He lifted the cover to reveal a perfectly plated meal, with toast and jelly.

"Please ring if you need anything." He backed out, almost bowing.

I put the cover back over the food. I'd lost any appetite I might have had. The coffee, however, was quite good.

When I was fourteen, still commanded by my mother to attend to the bathing of my younger sister, Lydia, while mother drank in the living room, a fire had somehow begun in my first-floor bedroom. It had quickly spread over the lower level. I didn't know anything was wrong until she screamed for me to get Lydia, get downstairs and out of the house. I don't know why I didn't smell the bitter acrid smoke.

Doris Day swished into the room with a black medical bag. She was all smiles and soothing voice. She propped up my feet on the other chair and then knelt, opened the bag and extracted a shiny scalpel that came with the antiseptic smell of camphor and mercurochrome.

"Whoa, there, Silver," I said, pulling my knees up. "What are you thinking here?"

"We need to first remove the dead tissue," she said. "I promise it won't hurt. Then we'll get some analgesic lotion on, then bandages. It will surprise you how fast you heal."

Against my will, I straightened my legs and she began her labors. She was right, it tickled – compared to the pain I'd suffered.

"What's with the gold?" I asked, downing the last of my coffee.

"Well, let's just say that the original owner of this house — the one who built it with his own hands, a country doctor by trade, an immigrant from Germany, was well read in alchemy and other arcane practices. When he finally discovered the secret, he knew his life was set. And all his ancestors. Doctor Dracovich is a great-great-nephew."

"What secret?"

As if she was speaking to herself, she went on to tell me the history of the house and its occupants over the years. Dr. Horace

Helmlik, the country doctor she had referred to, apparently had discovered the long-sought after method to change lead into gold. He had wisely kept it a secret, she said. It funded the construction of the Manor house and several outbuildings, one serving as his lab, which were all now gone, torn down or fallen in on themselves.

Horace died rich. His son, Frank, practiced medicine in the early 1900s, even though he had no formal training. He married a high society woman named Thelma who gave him two sons, both of which died young – one of tuberculosis, the other in the Great War. Frank, nonetheless, continued his father's alchemical research and experimented with new anesthetics and gold therapy for rheumatism. And also, Doris said, he explored biology and chemistry and the occult. Seances were held regularly, she said, in the great room. When he died – what we now call dementia - Thelma carried on as before, living high in her society circles, the object of many photographs in local newspapers.

"How does Dr. Dracovich fit into all this," I asked.

"He came to America in 1938 on the scientific wave of defecting German scientists. Trained in Chemistry and Biology, he failed to connect with the Project as the effort to build the bomb was known in Iowa at the time."

She said he filled in at the local college, mostly as proctor. His heavy accent and difficulty with language prevented him from his rightful place, so he often proclaimed. He managed to find his way here and the aging Aunt Thelma ensconced him as more or less a caretaker of Helmlik House. Before Thelma passed, he had learned fluent English and had read most of the books contained in the more than three thousand volumes the library has amassed, had learned the lessons of his ancestors and to degrees, carried on their work.

"Can I see him?"

"See him?"

"The doctor. Like, I need a signature?"

"Yes. Well, yes," she said. "I'm sure we can arrange that. I'll check his schedule and let you know."

"Ow! What the hell?" I felt like a drill bit entered my right foot. "What the hell?"

"There's no need for language, Ms. Bennington. It's just a suspicious skin lesion. It's gone now. Very little bleeding actually." She tweezed up a dark fleshy erasure-like thing and dropped into a vial she'd lifted from the bag.

"Motherfu…."

She next pulled a large glass tube from her bag of tricks and affixed a huge silver needle to it. "Let's get those blisters drained, shall we?"

I expected it to hurt but it didn't. While she engaged herself with sucking out thin bloody fluid and squirting it into other vials, she told me that the Doctor has health issues of his own and that when I see him, I was to act as if nothing at all was wrong. "He has," she said, "let himself go in his old age. Yet he wants nothing more than to live forever."

She went on to tell me that the doctor is quite the Renaissance man: Banking, day-trading, basic science chemical development for big pharm companies. "Have you heard of Femgo?" Well, duh? The female Viagra?

"As you have seen, he's a skilled taxidermist and has clients from all over the world who ship their bounty here. I'm surprised you aren't aware. How long have you lived in this town?"

I said nothing.

I heard a noise from in the hall and a door close. A man with a suitcase walked by without looking in and passed just as fast. I rub my unbelieving eyes. The man looked just like Harry Bellefonte. I know his face! My mother collected his albums. Felice Navida and all that. But it wasn't him. This Harry Bellefonte had a huge purple nose. A W.C. Fields nose.

"Are there other guests here?"

"Oh, no, she said. "We closed to the public soon after Doctor arrived." Her right eye did that funny thing, like a dust mote had gotten in it.

A wave of lightheadedness came over me accompanied by a sickly smell of something, a stomach acid smell. Doris began to gently rub my feet with a brown cream. In that moment, all pain in my feet disappeared.

She smiled when she saw the cream had worked. Her right eyelid drooped.

"The storm isn't letting up until late tonight. I'm afraid you'll have to spend another night here. You'll be down in the Library Bedroom tonight. Doctor is working on a new…a new specimen for his Collection Room. We've already moved your stuff down there."

She stood and smiled. "I've instructed Mr. Gilcrest to show you the way and have a brunch set for you at noon." She made to leave.

"What the hell do people do around here for fun?"

She turned, her skirts swirling like she was dancing. "Oh, there's plenty to do. You're free to go exploring if you want. Not to mention plenty to read."

With another eye twitch, she turned and left.

Sure enough, within a few minutes, Mr. Gilcrest introduced himself. He seemed normal, except his hands each had six worm-like fingers.

I felt anything but normal. My head swam around. My feet, now feeling no pain – could hardly detect the presence of the floor. A wave of nausea flowed over me. He escorted me down to the first floor, I held tight to the banister. The musical notes of Fleur de Les started up. He led me past a room with various horn and stringed instruments and there was the hunched Doris, her face held in consternation at the keyboard. Something was different about her head. A ridge of flesh or something. I rubbed my eyes – my vision had blurred. Nothing seemed right.

An egg and meat sandwich and potato chips had been laid out atop a table that seemed more like a table where people might study or confer. Mr. Gilcrest slithered away soon enough, leaving the door open.

The room seemed to expand, twice the size of the taxidermy room and again, golden-framed paintings encircled it. I noticed a small ancient bathroom without a tub through a door on one side and two closed doors stood in the center of the opposite wall. One look at the food and my stomach threatened to explode into my throat. With a steadying hand against a wall, I edged around the periphery.

I seemed in a daze. Drugged. Like waking up in the hospital so many years ago. The two of us - my mother and myself - had been severely burned and had to be heavily sedated. My sister Lydia had…she never made it to the hospital.

The largest painting was of a slim man in a hat, caught ministering by candlelight to a child at a bedside, his black doctor's bag at his side. A gold plate affixed to the frame was engraved: Horace Helmlick. M.D. (1841-1910).

Beside it, the visage of his son, Frank, also in doctor garb. The plate read 1867-1932.

I saw all this in a dreamy fog.

To the right, Frank again, now in a top hat, captured with, according to the plate on the gilded frame, Thelma. Both appeared to be somewhere in their forties.

Then, a series of grainy photographs, also in golden frames, although miniature in comparison, was their son, Helmitt, outfitted and posed with weapons of trench warfare.

And there again was Thelma, painted standing alone on the high railing of a tall building in what must be New York City.

The last, hung apart from the others, a painting of a heavy-set man working over a table of laboratory glasswork, bubbling liquids, notebooks, his white coat draped out of the picture below. Unlike the others, it was an enlarged photograph, in color and no doubt done professionally. He was handsome in a curious way, eyes alight with secrets and curiosity below high-arched bushy brows. Hair mussed, his head a triangle accentuating his sumptuous cheeks and billows of jowls, escaping over his buttoned-up white collar. Dr. Frederick Dracovich.

There was one more. Not a portrait or a photo, but a plaque that conferred upon Dr. Dracovich the Key to the City of Dubuque, framed skeleton key and all.

Books in the shelves, thousands of books. Despite the sudden urge to sleep, I browsed through some titles. From modern bound journals on cell biology and cloning and stem cell research, and one called "The Aging Human Animal," to old tomes with names like "Notions of the Afterlife" and "The Alchemist's Essential Guide," to a range of others about financial and exchange markets, anesthetic medical practices, and regeneration biology. A scientific journal lay over a small desk: *Longevity*.

Dizziness fell upon me. I sat. Had I been drugged? I hadn't eaten anything, maybe that was it. I needed food?

I made my laborious way to the tray of brunch and willing the nausea away, sat and scarfed down the sandwich and washed it all down with the coffee, now cool.

It had tasted wonderful earlier, hot, but now the room temperature brew had an unmistakable hint of herbs of some sort, and a bitterness I hadn't appreciated before. Drugs? I couldn't believe that. Why would they…

The machine, wherever it was, started up. Clanging and buzzing and whirling, as before.

I rose and went to the door. There was no one in the hallway and I made my lightheaded way to the stairs and down, thinking of getting the fuck out of there. Through the windows, the snow was letting up. I needed to leave.

I stopped at the second-floor landing where the noises were loudest. No one was about so I crept up the hall to a pale green door and listened. A smell of roses and something like wet dirt, maybe something dead emanated from within along with a sense of heat. I laid a hand on the surface, and it felt soft instead of hard, reminding me of the preternatural feel of the dead animals, as if the door itself had once been a living thing. And, yes. Warm.

From behind and below, I heard a clinking of glass and I got myself down the hall fast and pushed through the only door that I just knew it had to be locked but wasn't. A closet of sorts. From there, through a crack, I watched Doris go through and into the room carrying a tray of food and beverages. She left the door ajar.

My vision swimming still, I crept up on it and looked in. I had to.

What I saw was so astounding I first thought it was the drugs or whatever had caused my current discombobulation. Doris stood ten feet away, back to me. In front of her was a man floating in the air – levitating! A huge man sitting like a Buddha on a magic carpet of empty air. Naked save a gigantic diaper draped over the mile or so of his hips. His skin was slick with oil or sweat and draping mounds of glistening fat gave his body a sense of rolling away to the ground. It was without a doubt Dr. Dracovich, he of the arched eyebrows. The rest of him was nearly obliterated in massive morbid stinking obesity. His skin was thin, almost translucent, and gave off an eerie green cast, as if coated in a thin layer of bile, but also a blue electric spitz, like hummingbird feathers. The smell of dead things pressed in on me.

He reached one undulating massive arm up and clicked some square contraption obscured in the other hand. Electric motors kicked in and gears and pulleys and wires began to dance over his head. His gross corpulent frame I now saw was suspended in a swing that now was transporting him around the cavernous laboratory. In another age, it might have been the ballroom but now, it held six computers and wall screens and lab benches and an array of fucking plants and caged animals the likes of which I had never once seen. And a body – a female form laid out on a long table covered by a sheet.

I turned and ran on wooden feet. Enough of this fucking fun house!

My numb feet carried me toward the stairs down but the sudden image that sprang up before me caused me to pull up short. My feet gave way. I slipped. I banged my head into the top banister.

*   *   *

When I came to in the four-poster bed, sunlight was streaming through the small window. Morning light. Sunday, then. I felt drugged still, slow and akilter.

My head pounded. Like a video file, the memory I experienced at the top of the stairs replayed itself: of a long-ago explosion of vivid flickering orange, of trying to contain my slippery naked panicked little sister, of losing my grip, of…

I had to get out of that house. I was in the sweat clothes I'd been given. My socks and shoes were nowhere to be found. I hurried as best I could, on feet now painful again. The door was locked, of course. From the outside. I turned to the two other small doors that led off the room. The bathroom, but the others, all locked. I wanted to yell. Fucking bastards. Fucking crazy people. Let me out!

Then, I saw the key…The award! Could it be? I grabbed the frame and pulled it down and in one sweeping motion, broke the glass on the corner of the table. Digging with my nails, the skeleton key came loose from its tiny wire supports. I shoved it in the lock of the first door.

Nothing doing. I tried the second door. Goddam, no go. I threw the key across the room and sat, tears bubbling over my cheeks, swearing under my breath. Heat raged through me. Assholes. What did they want with me? I made a fist and punched the table, making the coffee cup splash over. Drugs again? Where my fist hit, dust sprang up, yet the table was spotless. I hit it again and more dust. I looked at my right hand, my red, red hand. There were whiffs of not dust but smoke coming off the skin! I held it to my cheek and immediately pulled it back. It felt as if it was on fire. Both my hands, I realized. I ran to the bathroom and ran cold water over them. They hissed for a second and the redness and heat slowly abated. Then, to my horror, the familiar ugly brown nib of flesh on my right hand – my worry wart that had served me all my anxious life – was no longer there. As if it had never been.

Before I could think about it, I heard the tinkle of glassware, silverware, from outside the door. Panic filled me. My first thought was to ambush Doris and hold her hostage, but I was drugged still, unsure of my footing, my movements. My ability to react.

Not thinking, I ran to one of the other locked doors and yanked and then kicked at it. I felt myself getting hot. I thought, *fucking right I'm hot.*

Another thought then, so simple and so perfect. I lifted the rug on which I stood and there it was. Of course. A key! In a second, I was through the door and pulled it behind me, locked it behind me, turning that ubiquitous little knob.

A short hall led to a narrow stairwell going up and down. Down, of course. A couple of bare light bulbs on bare wires lit the area dim yellow. At the first floor, I was about to storm out when I heard voices behind it. Waiting for me? Fuck.

The stairs led down to a cellar. I heard noise from below but what choice did I have? The door there was unlocked and I propelled through. A single oil lamp lit the space. While my eyes adjusted, a grating sound, a clickety-clackety.

There, before me materialized a dozen people walking around in a circle. People connected to a wooden harness over their waists which then hooked up at a central wheel, turning it like…like an old mill. Or a generator.

Their dead eyes paid me no notice. I crept forward. Each had a clear tube, a half-inch in diameter at least, connected to their neck, through which streamed a shimmering metallic liquid, shimmering greens and blue. Like the doctor's skin.

Then, I saw their faces. There was the face – not the face I saw before but the real face of Harry Belafonte. And behind him, the walking fucking zombie effigy of Doris Day, perfect, no hunchback. Next, a man I didn't know but that reminded me of Frank from the portrait, Horace's son, and next, Mr. Fields, the cook, but tall and handsome, not short and elephantoid. What the hell?

Freaked out, I looked around for a way out. I heard voices coming down the narrow stairs. I saw a tiny light on the other side of the room. An outside door? I ran for it, best I could. Halfway there, I noticed the merry-go-fucking round had gone round. The next three figures walked unseeing, rote, one after another, all of then Frank Dracovich. The first was the man in the portrait only more obese. Behind, the next Dracovich was coated in waves of fat, as if he'd fallen in upon himself. He trudged ahead on fat short legs; a lower lip that protruded and leaked that multicolored liquid. The last, tied with a rope to the one in front, was so fat it had been tethered and relegated to a wheeled cart, beholden to the others to bring it round.

I screamed. I couldn't help myself, because behind green fat Drakovich walked a young woman pushing the cart forward. A woman in a brown USP delivery outfit, her right hand blemished with a wart between the thumb and the index finger.

I screamed again. I ran toward the light. On the way, I clipped the oil lamp and it fell. Flames burst from a stack of cardboard below. But I had to move, had to get out.

I forced my way through an ancient rusted coal shoot to the outside, to be clear of the house, to scurry and fall, and then get up again, and tumble through the melting snow and finally back down the path, shooting backward glances all the way to my truck– thank God – my waiting truck.

Two weeks later, my feet were almost back to normal. The plastic surgeon didn't need to see me again.

I wasn't, though. Wasn't normal. Ever since, I didn't feel like I used to, Didn't feel like the old me.

I told the receptionist I didn't need another visit. I was released. She asked for payment. She showed me the bill. It was outrageous! I probably hadn't made that much money in my entire life!

I couldn't help myself, even though I'd gotten back on my Adderall.

"No fucking way I'll pay that! Who the hell do you guys think you are? Star quarterbacks or something?" God, I was hot!

I awoke that next morning feeling some better. I stopped for coffee and saw the Dubuque Telegraph Herald on a ledge. The headlines freaked me out.

WEST FOLLOWELL SHOCKED BY TWIN FIRES: SURGEON PERSIHES

Below that: ARSON SUSPECTED.

The Decay Diary
Michael Roby

One:

The world as we knew it ended March 27th, 8:23 AM, Central Time.

I woke up twenty minutes before my six AM alarm and wasted the chance for more rest on my phone. As I scrolled through our YouTube channel, my bulldog rose from his spot at the foot of the hotel bed and inspected the edge.

"Xavier, over here." The whisper was force of habit, there was nobody else in the room to wake up.

My knobby-legged little dog looked to me, ears raised, like he couldn't believe I was already awake. When I turned back to my phone, he walked right up next to my head and plopped down. His glance and deep sigh seemed, as they often did, judgmental.

"Hey, leave me alone," I said. "I'm getting ready for the day in my own way"

Views on our latest videos weren't terrible, but engagement was in decline. It felt like I watched the soul drain out of the channel as I scrolled from older videos to new. Eight months before, our name changed from, "The Decay Diary" to, "Zahra, Kurt, and Abandoned Places." I felt like that was where things really went downhill.

A minute after I turned off my alarm, my phone buzzed. A profile picture of a curly-haired, bearded man with a goofy grin popped up.

Todd: Kurt's already up and kinda pissed. Maybe grab breakfast on the go so we can get moving?

My glance turned into a glare. I started and deleted a couple different replies. They ranged from, "Tell Kurt tough, I need to shower," to, "He can keep walking over you, but he's not gonna do it to me." Last, I considered a lengthy dissertation about the routines of proper Afro care. At some point I decided I'd written off most of the day's trip anyway. With a long, disgusted sigh, I replied, "Be down in a few."

Within the next five minutes I threw on a T-shirt, jacket, blue jeans, and deodorant. With Xavier's leash clipped on, we stopped at the hotel's little breakfast nook and threw together an egg sandwich. The chilly breeze and cold mist that hung outside reminded me it was still technically winter. I led Xavier over to the grass and started on my sandwich. He turned to look at me, I nudged him. "Do your business, then maybe you'll get some."

He whined and took a few steps into the grass. During a bite of my breakfast, my phone buzzed. I intended to ignore it and send a message later, but it kept buzzing. My annoyance mounted; Todd was trying to call me. I still wanted to ignore it, but I was stuck with these people the rest of the day. I didn't want to make things worse. "Hello?"

"Hey, Zahra, where you at?"

"In front of the hotel, trying to get Xavier to piddle before we're driving for the next forty minutes."

"Ah. Right. Probably a good call." Todd hesitated before he continued, and because it bothered me, I lowered the phone a little. "Well, come to the car soon as that's done."

"I think I can hear you." We'd parked on the side of the hotel, so couldn't see the car, but there wasn't any other noise in the way. "Are you waiting outside."

"Kurt, uh, well, he wants to get moving."

I swallowed another bout of anger; Todd didn't deserve it. The worst he was ever capable of being was a doormat. He didn't want to be up this early or headed for the car any more than I did. Kurt had to be egging him on. But for all I told myself that, I didn't have it in me to text it.

Xavier gave me a squat, I rewarded him the last bite of the sandwich, picked up after him, and crossed to the side of the building. Todd leaned against my blue Ford sedan and fiddled with his camera. Olive toned, blue-eyed, blond Kurt towered over him and stood straight, arms crossed. He didn't pretend to be busy with anything but waiting and trying to glare through his sunglasses. As tall and muscled as Kurt looked on camera, I understood how he helped bring in new viewers. Hell, I didn't used to mind it when people asked if we were dating in the comments. But that morning wasn't the first one he'd acted like an asshole from the moment I'd woken up.

Kurt did surprise me when he flashed a smile as we approached. "Hey, now there's our star." The feeling passed as he knelt down, opened a hand to Xavier, and scratched behind his ears.

"All right," Todd said, "Everybody ready to roll out?"

I unlocked the car. "Yeah, let's do this thing." Todd climbed into the front seat; Xavier followed me on the driver's side but hopped back with Kurt when I shooed him. "Todd, can you get the address pulled up?"

"Already on it."

"Maids were running the laundry all goddamn night and our room was right next to it," Kurt said. "So, if we can keep things quiet this trip, that'd be nice."

I spent the previous night in the only room with a double bed and a half-broken heater to save money. The latest videos we shot for YouTube suffered diminishing returns, and I didn't think that trip would change anything. Still, Kurt could go from annoyed to irate when contradicted at the wrong time. That fight didn't seem worth it.

All was quiet for the first seconds in the parking lot. Then the artificial British woman's voice from Todd's phone said, "Starting route to Monstrous Forest Funfair and Campground. This location is permanently closed."

Two:

Monstrous Forest Funfair opened in the sixties and survived five or six rebrands. At varying points it was an old west gulch, a medieval village, and a licensed Yogi Bear campground. By the time the park closed in 2009, the owners accumulated so much mismatched décor they painted goofy faces on everything and called them, "monsters." That all made for a decent story, but it felt out of our way for a dumb, gimmicky stop. Kurt and Todd outvoted me two to one though. Seemed to happen a lot those days.

Interstate directions eventually led to guidance through a small town. Roads grew worse with each mile, foliage in front yards gave way to forest. I hated being up so early, but as the tall, skinny fir trees grew denser, I was glad we wouldn't be driving back at night.

"Oh my God." Todd laughed. "Is that Grape Ape coming up on the right?"

I frowned. "Huh?"

Todd pointed. "Slow it down a bit, he's back in the trees."

With a foot eased onto the brake I squinted where he motioned. Some figure stood further into the forest. Half of the statue's head and an arm rotted away, and a sloppily painted face covered the thing's belly.

Camera raised and window down, Todd leaned out to capture some B-roll. "Very nice, very nice."

"What did you call that thing?"

"Maybe Grape Ape, maybe Magilla Gorilla, dunno. Old Hanna Barbera characters, might have gotten thrown in with the Yogi Bear deal."

An audible sigh slipped up from Kurt in the back. "What'd I say about a quiet ride?"

"We're almost there," Todd said. "We'd have to get you up in a second anyway."

Kurt groaned but uttered, "Fine."

I picked up the pace again, but soon the path went rocky and forced me to slow. After that, two poles stood up on either side of the road, like they once held a banner. Two halves of an old, rusty gate sat at the base of each pole, tangles of dead weeds and vines grew between them.

"Man, imagine if there was a big sign here." Todd chuckled. "Then think if every time they changed the theme, they just crossed out the old one and scribbled in a new name."

That got the first real laugh of the day from me. For the rest of the short drive, it seemed like things improved. The rocky road leveled out again and we turned into a wide, empty parking lot. A flight of stairs with weeds growing in the cracks led from the end of the lot up to a large building atop the hill. In bloody letters toward the top it said, "WELCOME" and halfway down it read, "ADMIN BUILDING."

I pulled Xavier's leash, led him out of the car and to the grass in case he needed another stop.

Todd stepped out of the car, camera in hand. "All right, folks, get your game faces on."

Kurt emerged, popped the top of a sports drink bottle with his teeth, and took a long gulp. When he finished, he let out an exasperated sigh, and threw the bottle back in the car. "Let's get this over with."

Before we took another step, Xavier went rigid, yanked on his leash, and barked at the building on top of the hill.

"Woah, bud." I pulled back on the leash to fight for control, but my dog kept up his barks and snarls.

Kurt looked between Xavier and the park. "What the hell's his problem?"

"Hang on, be quiet you guys," Todd said. "This freak out could help us sell on the creepy atmosphere."

In the middle of Xavier's barking fit, a swarm of fat, black birds blew out from the horizon and flew overhead.

"Getting back in the car," Kurt said. "I don't wanna deal with bird shit."

I stepped out of their path while Xavier kept barking. "What are they?"

"Turkey vultures, probably," Todd said. "They're scavengers and they're native. Must be a dead deer up there or something."

My face tightened. "We're not putting that in the video."

"A dead deer? No way," Todd said. "But if it's there, I should pry find it so we can keep it out of the frame."

The vultures flew past the tree line and left us again. I called, "Kurt, come on out, they're gone." I flipped my phone open. "Todd, you got any reception out here?"

Todd checked his own. "Nope. Truly in no man's land now." We ascended the stairs, the large administrative office waited at the top of the hill. It looked like a simple brick building hastily covered with art of ghosts and three-eyed, four-armed monsters. A playground with a rusty jungle gym and a tunnel painted to look like a dragon sat across from us. "God, this place is cheap," I said.

"Oh yeah." Todd nodded. "Total shitshow. That's what makes it fun. Let's check out the admin."

I kept my objection to myself and followed. Todd pushed through the unlocked front door where a, "Closed for the season" sign hung. Xavier and I followed right past the "No dogs allowed" sign and I tried a light switch by the door. Of course, nothing happened. Enough sun slipped in to show a messy room. Despite lingering cold outside, the insulation was good enough to make it stuffy. Todd crossed the paperwork-strewn floor and stepped up to a receptionist desk. A big, unreadable graffiti mark covered the opposite wall and assured us we weren't the first to come by. The thought Kurt might ask me to translate tied a little knot in my stomach. Maybe in solidarity, Xavier pulled as far as his leash would let him and raised a back leg toward the mark.

"Aw man, this is a treasure trove." Todd pulled documents out of a filing cabinet next to the desk and rifled through. "Come here, you and Kurt are gonna have to reenact finding this stuff later."

I stepped to his side and peered down. Brochures of the park's many iterations, some colorful, others old and faded, piled up alongside center-folded maps.

"No freaking way!" Todd laughed. "You gotta be kidding me, look at this."

He grabbed an ancient-looking pamphlet. At the center stood a happy cartoon family with mouths open in conversation. Around them were four walls detailed to look thick and metallic. A nuclear fallout warning sat stamped in the right-hand corner next to the words, "Baxter's Bunker Company Fallout Shelter Manual."

Todd flipped through the handbook. "I mean, this place was running back in the sixties, that checks out. There's some old, third-rate made bomb shelter around here. The northeast corner of the park, looks like."

I glanced at one of the maps he'd pulled and, against all my frustration, chuckled. "Well, you're really not going to believe this. Back when the park was Robin Hood themed, they started using it as a dungeon."

"No! No, they couldn't possibly—" Todd leaned in and looked at the spot I held my finger over. Right along the river that formed the park's northeast boarder was a mark for Prince John's Dungeon. "That is amazing."

For a moment at least, I felt glad someone was having fun.

"Ugh, why the hell's it so hot in here?"

I deflated as Kurt stepped up to the desk.

"Find anything we can work with?"

"Yeah," Todd said. "Let's leave the door open and get a couple pickup shots outside, should cool things off."

Three:

As soon as we started shooting again, Kurt found a fight to pick. As we left the building and approached the playground, Todd asked. "What do you think, Kurt? Gonna get into some dragon guts?"

Kurt scowled at him. "What?" There was nothing playful in his voice.

"Y'know, over in the play area." Todd waved. "You gonna take a crawl through that tunnel?"

He turned away. "Piss off."

"Hey, take it easy." Todd lowered his camera. "That's usually your character, right? You love being a goof for the audience."

"Well maybe I'm sick of acting like some brat."

"Kurt, I'm sorry, I—"

"Well, you're bullying Todd like some brat right now."

Kurt turned his look and fury toward me, maybe in shock at my audacity to raise my voice at him. "Both of you, piss off." He trudged toward the playground and sat down on top of the tunnel, arms folded.

I glared at Todd. "Don't you dare record any of this."

With his free hand raised in surrender, he turned away. "Wouldn't dream of it. I'm gonna find somewhere to take a leak, shout when it's over."

"Here, take Xavier then." I passed off my dog's leash, Todd accepted it without saying anything. Arms folded, I stepped up to Kurt.

"Don't bother saying anything." He didn't look at me. "I'm not going in this stupid thing."

"And you know what? We don't even have to film that it's here," I said. "But we both know that isn't the episode's biggest problem right now."

"No?" His tone mocked me.

"You've been acting like an asshole since I got up this morning—since you got up this morning too, according to Todd."

"I got a bad night's sleep." Kurt still wouldn't look at me.

"I think it's a lot more so that you don't wanna be here."

"Yeah, no shit. Do you wanna be?"

"I voted against it," I said.

"Oh, quit rubbing it in. I get it, this place sucks. Maybe it'll pick up some views anyway, but I'm not holding my breath."

Something in my gut told me I should say we could hurry and wrap up the shoot. And something louder told me not to give the big baby his bottle. "I think it's about time you stop dragging us to these places then."

Kurt stood up straight, looked down, and it felt like he wanted to cut me in half with his glare. "And I think it's about time you remembered your place here."

His size made me want to back away, but his words solidified the cement that held me in place. At my most furious and disgusted, I asked, "My place?"

"I'm the one who stopped uploading to my channel, Todd was working for me before he'd ever heard of you. We joined your show and we've driven up your views ever since."

"You've been driving up views because you push for shallow garbage like this," I said. "Viewership's up, but engagement's down. Nobody leaves comments anymore because you and Todd always wanna go for this dumb bullshit. For God's sake, you dragged us to a closed down Discovery Zone last month so you could mug from around the corner—"

Kurt stepped forward, palms open. "Back off!" And shoved me.

I lost my footing and fell, grit and spiney plants bit into my palms, but they hardly registered. My blood dropped ten degrees. A few boyfriends put their hands on me like that before, and it was always the last straw. The cold in my veins turned to fire as I pushed up, fists clenched, all thought of consequences gone. "Who the hell do you think you are—"

8:23 AM arrived. The world as we understood it died and roared into rebirth before we could process anything. Whatever else I wanted to say toward Kurt died in my throat. The way he froze, his face twisted in confusion, and then looked up, I knew he noticed the same sudden change I had. We both understood something was unfathomably different, but neither articulated it.

"Uh, guys," Todd said as he approached. "What the hell happened to the sky?"

Four:

Todd saw it too. That meant I didn't imagine it. Oh God, that meant it actually happened.

In the instant of change, the color blue completely disappeared. The sky took on a deep yellow shade like dried mustard. I grounded myself enough to feel all over my body, I had to ensure a new, horrific instinct wasn't real. Jacket: red. T-shirt: white, jeans—

My jeans were the same nasty, crusted yellow as the sky.

I turned toward Kurt. "Kurt," I said. "Can you— could you— take your glasses off?"

He gawked for a moment. I still don't think he understood what I wanted when he pulled off his aviators. A gasp escaped me and my stomach churned.

"What?" A frantic tone took his voice. "What's your goddamn problem?"

"Y-y-your eyes."

"Holy hell." At some point Todd stepped up behind me. "They aren't blue anymore either."

"What?" Kurt turned his aviators around and tried to make out his reflection. Even from where I stood that same hideous yellow was clear looking back at me.

"This— this isn't right," Todd said. "This has to be a weather thing, or—"

I took another step backwards and bumped into Todd. I turned around and a scream rushed out my throat. I ran toward Kurt before I faced him again.

"Jesus, Zahra, what's wrong?"

"What— what—"

Kurt took over. "What the shit happened to you?"

"Huh?" Todd said. "What are you talking about?"

I still couldn't find words. Kurt shouted, "Where the hell is the rest of you?"

The camera with Xavier's dog leash floated opposite us without Todd gripping it. The lens lowered and looked left and right like a head shaking. Then it jerked up. "Oh my God, no! Where's my body? How am I holding this?"

"What kinda evil thing is going on right now?" Kurt pulled his glasses back on and searched around. "I swear if this is some joke—"

I tried to ignore him and approached the floating camera. "Todd, I'm sorry, it's weird for us too, but can you feel this?" I ran a hand around the sides of the camera without making contact and met no resistance.

"No," Todd said. "I—I couldn't feel anything."

With a hard swallow, I laid a hand on the lens.

"Oh my God." Todd's voice went high, like he was about to sob. "I felt that though."

Todd became the camera. The thought felt sickening and ridiculous as the disappearance of the color blue. But both horrors seemed to be the new reality.

As I struggled to wrap my head around everything, a scream of, "ROT!" echoed from behind us. We turned as one shout gave way too many repeats. "ROT! ROT! ROT!"

"Screw this, screw all of this," Kurt said. "Let's get outta here."

For the first time all day I was ready to agree with Kurt. But when I turned to follow, amidst the shouts of, "ROT! ROT! ROT!" Xavier slipped into a fit of his own. At a run he pulled on his leash until the weak knot around camera-Todd's handle slipped free and he rushed off.

"Xavier, no!" I ran after him. Even with his stubby legs, he was always faster than me.

Kurt shouted, "Leave the stupid dog!"

I ignored Kurt and rushed after Xavier. My dog dashed past picnic shelters and tiny shacks made to look like monster's heads. Xavier pushed beyond them all, but even those cheap effects slowed me down for a moment. Had the management of this crummy park gone to really carved points into the teeth at the front doors? And had they used some kind of white paint that glistened, to make the fangs look wet with saliva? I tried to force away more frightening possibilities. As we ran, the shouts of, "ROT! ROT! ROT!" grew louder.

Xavier finally yielded at the edge of the woods. With a skid I brought myself to a stop and stepped on his leash to keep him in place. I meant to scold him, but the chants kept coming too fast and loud, I knew I'd be overtaken. From there I finally saw what made the noise. The same flock of turkey vultures circled over a patch of dead trees a ways into the forest. The stink of an animal corpse hit me a second before I saw the tight, leathery remains of a buck on the yellowed grass. I leaned down and picked up Xavier. It seemed I'd only imagined they said, "Rot" and it was the noise of those birds. With a sad look at the deer, I uttered a silent prayer for its spirit.

Then the leathery skeleton jerked about and let loose an agonized, throaty cry.

"No way—it can't be," I said. The creature looked like it laid there dead for weeks. How could it be so decomposed and yet—

One of the turkey vultures called out, "ROT!" and descended. The bird landed on the buck's broad horns and bent down, probably to peck at his eyes. But then the bird jerked, hissed, and screamed. Its black feathers turned gray within a blink and then molted off. The vulture lost its balance, fell to the ground, and a second stink joined the first. The vultures overhead looked down on this and their chants changed. "BAD ROT! BAD ROT!"

Vomit rose in my throat, but I forced it down. Xavier wriggled in my arms; I held him tight as I could. I stared both in horror and struggled comprehension into the forest. Seconds later, something else caught my attention. The tips of blades of grass and brown leaves seemed to end in an arc shape and gave way to new greenery and trees just past the two bodies. But the longer I observed, little by little, the line of dead grass and dying trees seemed to approach me. It didn't take long to appreciate the difference, and I came to another horrific conclusion.

The sound of footprints on grass called from behind, I turned to see Kurt and the floating camera puffing. "Ugh, damn dog," Kurt said. "What's that smell?"

"I just saw one of those birds go from alive to dead of old age in a second," I said. At once I felt in control of myself again and backed away. Xavier remained tucked under my arms, and the invisible barrier that killed the vulture continued to inch closer. "The park—the whole park is decaying."

"What are you talking about?" Todd—it was still so disturbing to think of the camera that way—said. "What's going on?"

"I'll explain later. We need to get to the car, now." I took off at a run toward the admin building and the hill we'd first climbed. Mentally, I tried to figure how I'd explain what I'd seen. At least some of the bizarre events we'd encountered had a kind of awful, twisted logic to them. I couldn't come up with why blue was gone. But our camera man became a literal cameraman, the birds probably said the exact same things as before, I could just understand them. And the park was, quite literally, in a state of decay.

With my feet going sore and my breaths heavy, I reached the admin building and looked down. My heart sank and my stomach turned. At the bottom of the hill my car lost its blue sheen and become another thing of the sky's sickly yellow. But worse than that, the grass at the bottom of the staircase stood stiff, brown, and dead. Blade by blade, the grass up the hill died too.

"God—dammit." Kurt caught up and keeled down in a fit of puffed breaths. "Would you—quit running off—like that."

"We're trapped." My voice quavered as I searched around. As far as I could see, the decay formed a perfect circle and inched inward at us. "This whole place is dying."

Todd levitated to me and the camera lens moved left and right. "The grass—it's—and every second, more of it is dying, isn't it?"

I stepped back, my heart raced but the confusion and fear sapped any stronger motivation from me. "Kurt, do you see what we're talking about?"

"Yeah." He swallowed loud enough I heard him. "What if, I dunno, Todd tried to get down to the car?"

Anger flared in me again. "I don't know, because he's been through enough? Why don't you—"

"Zahra, wait," Todd said. "Kurt might be right."

I turned to the floating camera, blood still boiling and stomach still roiling. "What? Electronics can decay too you know."

"Yeah, yeah, but maybe it isn't the same," Todd said. "I have no idea what's going to happen, but we may as well know how the rules of this work, right? If I can escape, it could be the first step to figuring out how you guys can too."

Pain in the ass that Todd could be, I still didn't want anything—or anything else— to happen to him. Another objection fought for freedom but died in my throat.

As Todd turned away, Kurt called, "You're doing this for all of us." Somehow, after all that transpired, I hated him more than ever.

The floating camera gave me a nod by tilting his lens down and turned. Discerning exactly what steps Todd took was difficult, given I wasn't sure if he even still had feet. But at the appropriate moments for steps to be taken the camera rose then fell. As Todd approached the encroaching rot, his movements slowed, the floating camera extended to the end of a step and stopped. It was like Todd stood on a beach, waiting for the tide to come in and tell him if the water was cold.

Todd screeched and the camera jerked back up the stairs. "Oh God!" His voice went shrill. "I felt it, I felt it!" He sounded on the edge of tears and the camera flew at me.

I grabbed Todd as he rushed and cradled him under one arm. A thin layer of fiery rust covered one corner of the camera. Todd sounded like someone had just struck an exposed nerve and he could choke on his own gasps.

"Well, shit, what are we supposed to do now?" Kurt stepped forward and looked at the destruction as it advanced.

I shut my eyes tight, held Todd and pulled Xavier close, and struggled for another answer. Blue's disappearance felt like chaotic nonsense, but there was still strained reason to Todd's form and the screaming birds. Was there anything like those oddities that we could use to our advantage? If the world was ending—

"Todd," I said. "There's an attraction in the remains of that old fallout shelter, right?"

Five

An old map from the admin building in hand, we headed northeast. I felt thankful we couldn't see the encroaching decay as we moved deeper into the park, and I kept tight to the stonework path as if it could protect us. If my eyes stayed on the ground, I could almost pretend everything hadn't gone to hell. But it was impossible to keep the sky and its disgusting new look out of my periphery. And it wasn't more than a few minutes into the walk we caught echoes of, "ROT?" and "BAD ROT!" in the distance.

At the end of the path, we came to a rusty fence with a small, "Employees only" shack in front. I looked back and forth between the map and the barrier before I concluded, "The entrance to the shelter is back there."

Kurt didn't miss a beat, stepped up to the door of the shack and bashed it with his shoulder. The entrance gave a strained, pathetic *skree* and flew open. He stepped into the darkness, came back with a woodman's axe, and took a few swings at the rusted fence. Soon enough, our path looked clear.

As we walked past Kurt, Todd shifted his lens in his direction. "Uh, any reason you're holding onto that thing?"

"Bad enough the dirt is trying to kill us or whatever," Kurt said. "There could be something else here. Even just those birds could come at me. They're not gonna get me without a fight."

Given his nasty attitude earlier, the last thing I wanted out of Kurt was more macho man bravado. But we had to keep moving and he'd given voice to fear I carried too: there could be something else in the park blocking the exit. I held my tongue to resist an argument and we all pressed onward.

It was only a little further when we came to a narrow concrete staircase. At the bottom of the walkway, a heavy door sat cracked ajar. One sign screwed in said, "Outlaw's Dungeon." Above that hung another that again said, "Employees Only." I hugged Xavier close to my chest and turned around one more time. Kurt tapped the handle of the axe with his free hand. Todd, such as he was, stared ahead and gave me a nod. After a push, I took my first step into the darkness of the shelter.

A few steps in I jerked my foot back. "Shit!"

Todd asked, "What?"

"Cold—it's cold. And wet." I set my foot down again, it made a splash and icy water rushed into my sock. "Looks like the river flooded some of this place."

"Flooded?" Kurt's voice sounded high with paranoia. "Flooded how?"

"It must have sprung a leak overhead or something," Todd said. "We've gotta push on."

"Easy for you," Kurt said. "Your floating ass can't even feel any this, can you?"

Todd remained silent for a moment before he said, "I'd give anything have my body back, even now."

"Leave him alone, Kurt." I dug into my pocket and pulled out my phone. With a flip of my flashlight app, I illuminated the underground. A purple-skinned creature smiling a bloody grin sneered back at me.

I screamed and retreated backwards. Kurt ran out in front of me and swung his axe as Xavier barked. The head of the monster flew off with the sound of smashed plaster and fell into the ankle-deep water.

"What the hell was that supposed to be?" Kurt's shout made an echo through the passage.

After a few moments' hesitation, I shined my light at the decapitated head. When I illuminated up at the monster's body, it remained stiff. "I… I think it was just a decorative statue." With my phone raised I lit up more of the chamber. A dozen, maybe two dozen, other figures stood motionless in our path. "They must have been using this place as storage."

"Perfect opportunity for these damn things to come to life and attack us." Kurt gripped the axe tight and moved ahead. I exchanged another uneasy look with Todd. A moment later, Kurt called, "Zahra, make yourself useful and gimmie some light. My hands are full."

I'd have told him to adjust his attitude but was in no mood to argue with a man holding an axe.

The icy water leveled off around our knees, the journey into the shelter felt long and slow. Occasionally something, a blue-skinned Friar Tuck, or a Boo Boo with spider eyes, stood in our path. The weave felt easy for me, but Kurt caused many clatters and clanks. He shouted after each one, like he kept bumping into everything. At some point, mumbles started to slip out of Kurt's mouth and echo off the walls.

I turned. "Kurt? Can you see all right? Do you want me to bring up the rear?"

A spurt of laughter slipped from him. "Oh, you'd like that, wouldn't you? Monsters everywhere, and you'd be behind me. Where you could stick a knife in my back!"

I flinched. "What?"

"You can hear them talking too, can't you? And they know they can't take me alone; they need help to get me—"

"Kurt, you're talking crazy." Todd levitated toward him. "Come on man, it'll be all right, you gotta—"

A second too late, I shouted, "Todd, don't—"

Kurt roared and swung. "You're not one of us anymore!" The axe collided with the camera, and the sound of snapping plastic melded with screams. Todd fell into the water and burbling overtook his cries of agony.

"No!" I ran at Kurt and opened my arms to grab at the axe, Xavier slipped from my grip in the middle of it. With an adrenaline-boosted pull I yanked at the weapon and almost wrestled it from Kurt's hands. "You can't—I won't let you."

"Not one of us—" Kurt overcame the surprise that gave me my advantage, rushed forward, and smashed me against the wall.

A sting and a crack emanated in my skull; I saw stars as Kurt pressed the axe's handle up against my throat. I caught a few quick breaths, but the harder he pushed the weaker I became.

"A-and you." A stutter overtook him. "You always ruined everything. A-a-always ruining my damn show!" Spittle flew from his mouth and onto my face.

I kicked and shoved, but Kurt didn't slacken. I could take a shot at him if he pulled the axe away and took a swing, but it seemed he had no intention of doing that. Not when he could just hold the axe right where it was and choke me to death.

From the water, Xavier barked an attack declaration and sunk his teeth into Kurt's leg. Kurt shouted and shook. Without all his weight against me, I gave him a shove and ducked out of his chokehold. Kurt kicked my dog off of his leg, I scooped Xavier up and ran deeper into the darkness.

"Z-Z-Z-Zahra."

I turned, the shattered remains of Todd levitated just above the water, his voice garbled like a broken electronic.

"D-d-d-don't leave m-m-m-me."

Kurt yelled again, no words, just guttural fury. I grabbed Todd, shoved him under my arm, and ran. Heavy footsteps and splashing water filled the chamber. Kurt's moves followed after mine, if he and his longer legs caught me, I didn't think I could rescue all three of us. There was still no exit in sight and nothing but a statue-crowded path ahead, it could only end with one of us dead.

A small shimmer of sunlight cut through the darkness of the shelter. For an instant I considered turning around. If the cavern was compromised, we all were running into the death that consumed the rest of the park. But I didn't let up, not if I'd be dead one way or another. Rushing water drowned my steps as I reached a hole in the wall. The river that formed the park's boarder spilled in like a waterfall. Sunlight shimmered off something on my opposite side, I turned and saw a shield. Or maybe it was a cooking pot lid decorated to look like a shield. Either way, I had a purpose for it.

I set Xavier down with a, "Stay," and whispered to Todd, "Try to float above the water." Without my footsteps to drown them out, Kurt's splashes soon grew louder. I held the shield to the hole in the wall and prayed. "Please," I said to myself. "Please please please." If we'd escaped the radius of the park, I could show Kurt we were safe. He might stop. We could all leave—

The tip of the metal ran red with rust after a second of exposure.

"No." I shook my head and my heart hammered like it wanted to break my sternum. "God, please no."

Kurt screamed as he came into visibility and rushed at me, axe raised over his head.

I pushed off the wall and lunged at Kurt with the shield up and every ounce I could force from my body. The counterattack took him by surprise, and he yelped as I pinned him against the wall. I caught him with his raised arms and the back of his head held an inch outside of the shelter.

Kurt's kicks and struggles seemed normal for a second, but then grunts gave way to shrieks. The skin on his raised hands tightened, the hairs on the back of his head grayed and fell out. As the wrinkles crossed his face, a sting like a chemical burn ran up from the tip of my finger to my elbow.

I shut my eyes tight and fought to keep down a scream. Kurt's roars echoed in my ears as the blaze seared my arm. With my left hand still pushing for stability, I grit my teeth and maintained the hold as the evil force outside rotted the flesh from my right.

After the longest minute of my life, Kurt stopped fighting.

Stricken but desperate for closure, I opened my eyes and looked up. His skull wore a mask of leathery, decayed skin, shrunken so they couldn't cover his teeth anymore. Kurt's yellow eyes bulged in their sockets and jerked about, so he still had some control over himself left. But not enough to fight. I released my hold: Kurt collapsed like dead weight.

"Z-Z-Z-Zahra?" Todd floated just above the water and approached me. "Is… is he—"

The last of my strength gave out and I collapsed. Out of instinct I tried to use my hands to break the fall. When I did my rotted right one shattered, then disintegrated. A howl of agony ran out of me, I forced the stub under my armpit and clutched it to myself. Tears of pain and the terror of what I'd done ran from my eyes, and I rocked there for a few seconds. When I found composure enough to turn to Todd, I nodded.

Xavier laid his front paws on my knee and licked my remaining hand. I looked down at him and gave the tiniest scratch to the top of his head. Except for the hole in the wall, nothing but darkness surrounded us. In spite of everything, it still seemed we would die down there.

As the three of us sat, another voice, deep but quick, echoed through the corridor. "Oh boy, and they were just a few yards away from the exit. You ever seen anything like that, Hoo Hoo?"

A second voice with a British accent, said, "Indeed I haven't, brown one. Such a tragedy."

Todd said, "W-w-w-what—"

I yelled down, "Hello? Is someone there?"

"Oh no no, no talking statues around here," the first voice said. "That'd just be one of them, what do you call 'em, clichés."

Epilogue

It took us less than two minutes to reach a tiny crack of light in the wall, push it open, and see the outside world again. The sky still shone yellow, but the grass on the ground was green. I gave a weak toss to get the shield over the threshold and, when it didn't rust, Todd and I stepped outside.

"The sky is still gross," Todd said. "Do you think it's like this everywhere else?"

I shook my head. "I don't know, I lost my phone in the bunker. Maybe we'd have reception by now if I had it." A groan slipped out. "Or maybe all the cell satellites transformed into bags of oranges or something."

The three of us followed the faint sound of cars in the distance. Our walk wasn't long, but after all we'd already pushed past, it proved exhausting. Through trees and uphill we walked until we arrived at a quiet asphalt road. Before we'd had a chance to wave down a car, a pickup truck of that awful formerly blue yellow pulled over. With Xavier's leash in hand and Todd floating next to me, we approached the window.

At the front seat, the driver turned to look at us in a series of slow, jerking motions. I took a step back when I realized she had hair made of a long, thin black ropes, her skin looked malleable as putty, and her mouth and eyes were enormous.

"Oh my God, please don't freak out," she said. "I—I know how this looks." Her mouth wasn't even in synch with her words. "It happened to me right when the sky went yellow. I can't believe it, not everyone was affected?"

Todd said, "Trust me, we were all affected."

Several expression's flashed across the driver's clay face one after another before she settled again. "Well, get in. You folks looking for a ride somewhere?"

I let out a long sigh and said, "Anywhere."

A Traveler Comes By
Paula Bryner

Entering the inn, the traveler was like a ghost after walking a long time. The need for rest overwhelmed her like the smoke from the cooking fire ate up the air inside the room. Taking a place at the end of a rough-hewn bench, she removed a glove and began to crack the walnuts that were scattered on the table.

"You're hungry, friend?" The questioner across from her was heavy set, his face covered in the scraggly beard of a serf.

The traveler made no gesture of answer, preferring instead to concentrate on the walnuts.

"You need drink?" The inn keeper appeared at the table, her apron smelling of garlic and animal fat.

"He's not a talker," the serf said.

The inn keeper cocked her round head and looked down at the newcomer. The traveler was enveloped in a fur coat that made them appear as if they were more animal than human.

"Ale." The traveler spoke only after she swallowed the walnuts in her mouth.

"What's that?"

"Have you ale?"

"Barley ale."

"It will be fine. And bread." The traveler dug three rubles out of a pocket. "I can pay."

"We've boar stew as well, if you like."

"It will be fine."

"So, you do have a voice." The serf spoke again as the innkeeper walked away.

"Most of us do." The warmth of the tiny space was beginning to tell on her. The traveler pealed her fur coat off, standing to toss it onto the space next to her. The sleeve of her embroidered shirt pulled up without her notice.

"Hey!" The serf pointed at her arm. "You've the mark."

The others at the table turned to gawk. Two women and three children, all round-faced and bulbous, their eyes bugging out of their heads as they stared at the traveler.

She yanked her sleeve down with annoyance before straddling the bench again.

"Nicolai." The innkeeper returned with a tankard. "Stop pestering my paying customers."

"See it?" Nicolai grabbed the traveler's hand across the table, his square fist like a vice. "It is the mark."

"Let go of me." She struggled until her hat and kerchief slipped off her head, revealing her thick, black braid. "You have no right."

"Push her sleeve up." One of the women reached out toward Nicolai's fist.

The traveler punched the woman with her free hand.

"You bitch!" The woman screeched like an owl as she began to stand.

"Enough of that." Olga shouted at the eager family on the other side of the long table. As she bent down to the traveler, her breath stank of onions. "I am going to look at your arm."

"Not until this brute turns me loose." The traveler's dark face contorted in anger. "I've weapons. I will not be molested."

"Let her go Nicolai, you oaf." The other woman who was with Nicolai had a calm, melodic voice. "I need to see it."

Nicolai freed the traveler and a red mark bloomed over her wrist.

The calm woman reached out to push up the traveler's sleeve. Her sloe-black eyes grew wide as her finger stroked the indigo tattoo.

"It is true." Olga's voice was now soft, full of wonder.

"The wolf and the two arrows, crossed." The calm woman met the traveler's gaze. "You are of an ancient, healing lineage."

"Or a werewolf," the other woman said. She was holding her jaw where a purple bruise was beginning to form.

"It is of no consequence." The traveler adjusted her sleeve again. "It was done when I was very young. An error, I assure you. Olga, is that your name?"

"Yes." The innkeeper brightened at the recognition. Most of her regulars could hardly remember her name much less ask a civil question.

"I paid for bread and stew and a pitcher of ale, not a tankard. Where are they?"

Olga's chapped cheeks grew red with embarrassment. She eyed the table as if trying to assess any other lack, then she hurried back to the kitchen.

"Of course it is of consequence," the calm woman said. "You are a healer."

"I am not."

"Then your father."

The traveler drank and found the ale bitter but satisfying. She looked over the lip of the tankard at the eyes staring at her from all round the room and sighed, realizing there would be no letting go. She bore the mark, but these were the true wolves. "I am looking for a man."

"That is no answer." Nicolai laughed. "All women are looking for a man."

"He is a priest." The traveler's eyes narrowed.

"Our village has a priest," the calm woman said. "Father Ivan of God."

The traveler shook her head. "No."

"Here now." Olga appeared again, setting the stew, bread and beer on the table. "Why do you search for a priest?" Olga asked after a long time watching her guest eat. "Every village from here to St. Petersburg has one."

The tavern around them grew silent. Only the pop of the high fire on the grate in the corner and a strange squeak like metal parts needing oil rose in the hot, smoke-riddled air.

"He took the life of my sister."

"You are lying." The woman who had been punched spoke again.

"What is your name?" The traveler leveled her keen, odd eyes on the woman.

"That is Anna," Olga said. "Nicolai's wife."

"Figures." The traveler smirked and poured herself more ale. "Well Anna, call me a liar again and you will get more than a cuffing. Believe it."

Anna seemed to shrink into herself, but her gaze focused on the traveler like a rat waiting for a chance.

"Are you a healer?" The calm woman went back to her questioning.

The traveler picked up her wooden bowl and drank the last of her stew, then she wiped her mouth with the gray cloth on the table. Everyone around her waited for a reply as she finished her ale. The traveler met the calm woman's sunken eyes. She was taken for a moment by their urgent expression, then she shook her head no.

"You have the gift." The calm woman pleaded. "You could heal, if you troubled yourself to."

"My sister was the healer." The traveler began to collect her things as her eyes, gray with a hint of lavender like a sky pregnant with snow, swept the room. "The mark was given to me in error while she gave away all her boons to strangers, like you." The traveler's attention shifted to the innkeeper. "Have you a corner where I might sleep for a time? Just a few hours, by your leave. I do not need much room."

"I have." Olga crossed her arms over her thick chest. "It will cost you."

"How much?" Other options went through her head as she waited for the answer. There had been a hollow tree off the road, and she may have seen a cave before that.

"Your name." The sound of Olga's words made the patrons quiet again. They all, to one degree or another, were desperate to know who this woman was.

"Very well. My parents called me Xenia." She hefted her things to her other arm and raised her voice. "My sister was Varvara of Cherlov and the priest who took her life called himself Grigori. If you know of him, please tell me. I will not spread your confidence. Now, where may I sleep?"

The room remained quiet, except for the fire and the grinding metal.

"There is a nook behind the hearth." Olga pointed to the stone masonry that encased the grate. "You may sleep there."

"My thanks." Xenia put her head down and marched to the fireside, pulling back when she reached the hearth.

"It is just here." Olga was following her like a baby duck pads after its mother. "What is wrong?"

Xenia pointed to the dog in a cage that walked and walked, panting on a metal wheel. The wheel turned a spit that held a whole pig roasting over the fire. The dog looked unwell, tired and in want of care. Xenia tried to breathe normally as the wave of its pain ran through her like an upset of the gut.

"The animal turns the spit." Olga looked at the dog and it would not meet her eyes. "As if I should do it?" The innkeeper laughed, making the dog wince.

"She needs rest." Xenia croaked the words, feeling her head swim with heat and her mouth dry with thirst.

"Water."

"In a while. Come, I will show you where you may sleep."

* * *

Xenia found that she could not sleep with the sound of the wheel grating against the spit just feet away. It did not surprise her when the woman with the calm voice, smelling of ale and wrapped in a bear skin, came around the rock wall.

"Healer?" The woman whispered the word in the darkness behind the stones of the chimney.

"Do not call me that."

"I will call you anything you like if you will only help me."

For the first time, the traveler felt the woman's need. Away from all the others at the table with their mixed agendas of doubt, curiosity and hatred, she could now appreciate the woman's fear for her child.

"Please." The woman was close to tears and her breath came in little, unsatisfying gasps.

"I hear you." Xenia shifted under her coat. Her voice in the dim space sounded tired. "How old is your girl?"

"My child is sixteen by the count of our priest."

"Sixteen years makes a woman, not a child."

"I know, Healer." The woman dropped to her knees with a thud that made Xenia's joints ache. "But she is my child, my only girl and oh she is so sick."

"Did I not ask you to call me something else?" Xenia spoke through her teeth and she pushed herself toward the sad woman, their faces just inches apart.

The woman felt a rush of something cold, like ice water from a winter spring. She turned away, raising trembling hands that showed the scars of a life full of labor. "I am sorry. So sorry. Please."

"All right." Xenia drew a breath in the silence and then she realized that she no longer heard the metal wheel turning. "Show me then."

"Heal… forgive me. Lady?" The woman peeked around her hands and was surprised to see Xenia with her coat and hat on.

"Show me then." The traveler repeated as she motioned toward the door of the inn. "Take me to your only daughter."

The woman was so shocked that she remained on the cold earth of the floor, her knees singing in pain.

"Come, come. I can see that I will have nothing of rest until your child is looked at."

* * *

The woman led Xenia through the high snow at the edge of a pine forest to a small cabin built of the trees around it. Pine boards made up the walls and boughs of pine covered the roof. The door, painted red to welcome good luck, creaked when the woman pushed on it. Inside a room filled with men and women was hot and close. They all turned when the cold air blew in, making the lanterns tremble.

"Xenia of Cherlov." It was Anna who spoke first. Her jaw was now in a bandage tied at the top of her head so her speech was stinted, like the walk of a man whose leg is broken. "You came after all."

"You are surprised." Xenia stepped forward and touched the woman's jaw. Pain the traveler would not allow anyone to see shot from her chin to her ear. She looked away, toward the bed on the far wall and her arm fell to her side.

Anna's hand crept to her bandage. She tried to ask what happened to her pain but found herself unable to speak.

"It is the only bed we have, Lady." The mother hurried the traveler to where her daughter lay. "She and I share it."

"Where is your husband?" Xenia looked down at the girl whose bright, brown eyes stared up at her like the dog's had as it turned the wheel.

"He is dead." Nicolai stepped forward from the press of people in the room. "Dmitri was a woodsman. Irina still wears the pelt of the bear that killed him."

"You are Irina?" Xenia stripped off her coat as she spoke.

The mother nodded. "So is she."

"Then what ails you, Irina?" As she reaching out, a hand grabbed the traveler's. "Ah!" She whirled on the person, her wrist stinging and her lower abdomen jumping like a hare. "Do not touch me."

"My regrets, visitor." The man wore a priest's black robes with a beard just as black. His familiar blue eyes danced in the lantern light. "I thought to help you avoid illness."

The traveler felt made of stone. At last, the man that she had hunted like a wild predator for years stood with her. She wanted to cry out, to lunge forward. Instead, she stood staring, aware that he knew what was really wrong with the girl in the bed, just as he knew why her sister put a noose around her neck and jumped.

"Father Ivan says that no one should touch me." Irina chirped from under her bedclothes and a hush fell over the room that was too hot and stank of humans. "I am ill."

"She can speak." The mother looked at the priest. "But you said –"

"And it was so." Ivan seemed untroubled. "Until this woman drew near."

"You cannot talk, Irina?" Xenia looked down, her odd, gray eyes entering the girl's clouded mind like a medicine.

"I could not." Irina's gaze never left the face of the priest. "Father spoke it, and so it was."

"You see." Father Ivan's manner was like that of a defying angel fallen from Heaven.

"Better to rule in hell…" the traveler whispered.

"What did you say?" The priest looked at her with more care than before.

"I am praying." Xenia lied with aplomb as she turned back to the bed.

The people assembled stepped closer while this strange woman took the patient's hand.

Xenia had to steady herself with her free hand on the bedstead at the touch of this young woman. Her belly jumped again but this time she knew the cause. Her own uterus felt full and heavy, as if a stone was planted there. Just like Varvara. The traveler realized the hot breath of the priest on her neck, like a wind straight from the open portals of Gehenna.

"Everyone out!" Xenia whirled on the mass of people behind her, unable to tolerate all the thoughts in her head any longer.

"You give orders?" Anna laughed out loud. "This is not your house. Cure the girl of her odd malaise. Make her stop puking twice a day."

"I cannot." Xenia, feeling sick herself, let go of the young woman's hand. "I cannot with all of you about, distracting me."

"And how are we –"

"Enough, Anna." The priest barked at his congregant as if he, too, was tired of hearing her prattling. "You may all go. It is late and you should be at home. Tuck your children in and pray for their health as you pray for the health of our sister, Irina."

"Thank you for your prayers." Irina's mother sat on the bed, holding her daughter's hand and nodding to her neighbors as they headed for the red door.

Ivan of God shook people's hands and made the sign of the cross over them as if he were thanking them for coming to Mass. Xenia watch with suspicion, knowing without question that the priest was the cause of young Irina's misery. Just as he was the cause of the loss of Varvara, the Healer of Cherov.

When the room was empty, the traveler was at last able to breathe in. She gave young Irina a smile and then she looked at her mother.

"Will she be well now?" The hope in the mother's voice was like rain after a drought.

"She is not ill."

Both the woman and the girl, their faces so similar in the dancing light around them, looked mystified.

"Of course, she is ill." The priest stepped to the bed, shouting and thrusting his hand toward the girl. "Look at her, pallid and sunken. She does nothing but sleep and vomit. How will you say she is not ill?"

Watching the girl cower, as her sister once had at the sound of that voice, the traveler felt the pain that she fought to keep down. She turned away from the women and saw nothing but red. The screaming in her jaw and hands, her knees and elbows, made what was happening clear. She could not see it, and never had been able to, but she knew what it was.

Ivan of God's smug, angry expression disappeared like vapor from a boiling kettle. His jaw dropped and his shining blue eyes grew wide. The creature that turned on him was not a healing traveler. A witch had been put in that place, a woman with wolf's teeth and claws like iron nails.

"Father?" The mother could not see Xenia's face, but she saw the fear in her priest's eyes.

"You did this to her, Grigori." The wolf woman spoke in a deep, slow voice around her dripping teeth. "Just like my sister."

"I had no part in it." The priest put his hands up as if he could defend himself against this thing before him. "God, protect your own."

"You are not of God." The voice filled the space. "Sleep, Irina."

Against all the will they could muster, mother and daughter fell silent on the bed. Both were terrified, confused and then asleep as if someone had blown out a candle.

"Out, Grigori."

The priest heard the voice not just in his ears but in his brain, his heart and his liver. He turned and ran out the red door. The high snow, his long cassock and the deep darkness slowed him to almost a crawl. Despite the cold, he could feel the trickle of sweat on his neck.

Ivan of God, once known as Grigori, felt the frozen misery of the thing's talons as they ripped his back open like the spine of a freshly caught fish. He tried to call for help, but no sound came forth from his mouth. It seemed the monster would let him run a moment, then pull him back to maim him all the more.

The thing behind him grunted and laughed at the same time. Iron claws tore open his hide and wolf teeth crushed his skull. Gore speckled the snow while other predators, those of nature, gathered close to take advantage of whatever was left as the rampant monster tore the priest who could not keep his hands off her sister into ribbons of soggy flesh.

*   *   *

The traveler found the inn a quiet place in this early morning hour. She was dripping with snow which clung to her fingernails and shirt. Though cold to the point of shivering, she felt exultant as her wolf eyes, more capable in the dark than a human's, peered around the room. In the cage above the now cold grate, the dog sat wide-eyed. When the traveler drew close, her tail began to wag.

"There, sweetheart." The traveler put her hand up to silence the dog while she looked around the inn once more. "They shouldn't see us leave, should they?" She ripped the cage open with one hand and took the dog in her arms. "I know they will have a new victim in this miserable hell soon enough, but at least you are free. And so am I, if only a little." She smiled, feeling her teeth returned to human form. "There is so much more evil to undo."

The dog wagged her tail and licked the traveler's face as they walked out into the silver light of dawn where fresh snow was beginning to fall.

Station 13

Stewart Lethbridge

Black letters on white, rectangular signs. Two signs, each about forty yards on either side of the single entrance. Two gas pumps under a plastic awning. Wooden building, unpainted. The squat shack couldn't have sold but the minimal amount of groceries. Maybe a couple brands of soda, chips, and candy bars. Perhaps, a few quarts of oil.

Twice a day for the last two weeks, Dave Marteen had wondered what the inside of Station 13 looked like. He'd found a lonely rural house ten miles west of the small town of Sombrio, New Mexico, which was perfect for his needs. Long had he wanted out of the fast-paced and high-crime of Chicago, out of the cutthroat atmosphere of the city's third largest law firm. Shrewd investments paid off with a sharp uptick in the economy, and he cashed out before the inevitable downswing. He had enough to live on…but not in Chicago.

He bought the ranch-style house and hired on part-time at the town's abstract office, working a few hours every morning entering documents and hand-written text into the new computer database. The rest of his days, he spent enjoying the view of the great expanse of the New Mexico desert from his shaded back patio while contemplating the plot for the novel he always wanted to write.

If asked, he wouldn't have been able to say why Station 13 intrigued him. He'd seen aging, deteriorating, and abandoned places before. Hell, they were all over Chicago. However, this building caught his attention. Maybe because of its remoteness. It lay about two miles outside Sombrio, and never had Dave seen any vehicles at the pumps or parked near the front entrance. In fact, he'd never seen a vehicle for any employee.

The sign on the inside of the dusty window always read *open*. Dave didn't know if any light shone inside because the bright morning and noon sun blazed from the south, reflecting off the glass. Was the place even in operation?

The first two days driving to work, Dave barely paid attention to the desolate station. Only on the third day did he take a closer look while passing. Dust devils swirled and died in the stiff breeze. Dark and dusty windows gave no glimpse of the interior. The story of Schrodinger and that pesky cat came to mind. Station 13 was both open and closed at the same time…unless one were to enter.

On his way home that third day, he slowed but nothing seemed to have changed from the morning. More dust devils, but otherwise no activity.

The next morning, Dave slowed and turned into the property. Between the pumps and the front door, he stopped. The pumps were decades old with flip numbers behind the plastic window. Displayed was the price of the last fill-up. $13.13.

The store's entrance was plain, wooden framed with an actual doorknob instead of a push bar or pull handle and a small pane of glass that reflected the sun the same as the main window.

He drove on, but that noon he slowed again. Still, no change. No cars at the pumps, no proprietor outside cleaning or taking a smoke break. Nothing. He powered down his window. The desert heat invaded, overpowering his air conditioner. Wind spattered sand and grit against the windshield and brought the faint scent of smoke as if from a smoldering campfire.

Another week and a half passed. Each day, Dave slowed, turned into the station, and stopped between the pumps and the door. Each day $13.13 showed on the flip numbers. Each day, the sun reflected so brightly he couldn't see inside. Each day, the morning breeze speckled sand. Each day, for a few seconds, he smelled wood smoke.

One morning, Dave asked himself two questions. Why did he keep stopping every day and why didn't he go inside? Curiosity compelled an initial investigation but only from the comfort—safety? —of the car. The remoteness and loneliness of the place chilled him deep inside. He had a crazy notion that if he did venture through that wooden door, he'd disappear. His car would fade from existence and Station 13 would return to its never-changing atmosphere…or perhaps disappear into the ether, Dave its latest victim.

On the third Monday, Dave happened to glance at his gas gauge. Almost empty. He'd done some sightseeing over the weekend, exploring dirt roads that ran for miles over the flat desert terrain before petering out to nothing or ending at the remains of former settlements. Not even ghost towns, the adobe buildings all but crumbled, the land reclaiming its own.

However, he'd neglected to fill up the gas tank in Sombrio on his way home. That Monday morning, he estimated he *might* make it into town but didn't want to take the chance.

Station 13 appeared a hundred yards in front of him. Nearing, he remembered the weekend. He'd traveled in all four directions but never saw any other sister establishment. Where were the first twelve stations? Were there any numbered past 13?

Once again, as he'd done for almost two weeks, he slowed, pulled in, and stopped between the pumps and the front door. He pushed the button near the driver's door to pop open the gas tank cover, exited the car, and approached the pump. The price display window, the hose and nozzle, and the lever to initiate and stop the flow of fuel. The entire unit was so old it didn't have a slot for a credit card…which meant he'd have to pay…inside.

Trepidation increased his heart rate. He felt the dull pain in his chest. This is ridiculous, he thought. It's just a gas station. Okay, one out in the middle of freaking nowhere, New Mexico. The interstate had taken away most of the traffic, so he shouldn't be surprised he'd never seen any cars here. Why hadn't it closed down long ago, and how had it survived through the decades?

Dave unscrewed the cap, unhooked the nozzle, and activated the lever on the pump. The numbers flipped to zero and a switch snapped inside the bulk of the pump. He stuck the end of the curved nozzle and pulled the trigger. Would he even receive gas? Maybe the underground tank was empty. In addition to no customers, Dave hadn't seen any tanker or supply delivery trucks.

He glanced toward the front door. The morning sun's reflection was a yellow ball on the glass.

Seconds later, gas flowed, and the numbers flipped, the price adding up each second.

Dirt devils spun behind him. Sand pattered his face. A wispy odor of smoke tickled his nostrils.

Other than the soft chugging of the pump and the soft howl of the wind, there was no other sound in the desert. No car passed.

He was the lone traveler…as he'd been every day since he'd arrived in the Land of Enchantment.

Enchantment was right. The entire scene had a touch of the surreal, as if just off center of reality.

The nozzle coughed indicating back up of gas from a full tank. He replaced the cap and closed the cover. When he returned the nozzle to the pump, he noticed the price. $13.13.

He stared at the numbers, the same he'd seen every day. $13.13. Surely, he'd put more into the tank. Unfortunately, the price per gallon number had faded to obscurity.

He turned to the entrance of Station 13. If anything or anyone moved behind the window, he couldn't see. For a moment, he didn't want to go inside, but he had to pay. He wasn't the type to pump and run. In Chicago, he might have escaped. Not here. His car was too recognizable and wouldn't be difficult for authorities to track.

He chided himself for being scared. Frightened? It was silly. Just go pay and get to work.

The door creaked open, and he stepped inside. Shadows dominated the interior. One strip of dim, urine-yellow fluorescents provided the only illumination besides the sunlight through the windows. The rows of shelves held grocery items all covered in dust. Campbell's soup, saltine crackers, generic paper plates. In the back, a Pepsi machine that dispensed actual glass bottles occupied one corner. Next to it a stand-up cooler offered canned soda. Nehi and Fanta.

To his left, the check-out counter, waist high with a cash register the size of a small safe on one end.

Behind the counter was a man who, without the slight forward curvature of his spine, would have stood at least six-nine. Thin enough his drab faded brown clothes hung loose on his frame. Long, wrinkled face, sparse gray hair, deep-set eyes as shadowed as the aisles.

Dave stepped up and ruffled through a wad of bills from his front pants pocket. "Just the gas."

He found a ten and four ones and was just about to lay the money on the counter when a slurping-sucking sound emanated from the tall man. Not just from his mouth, but as if oozing from every pore. The desert-tanned skin darkened to a dark green mottled with bruise yellow pustule-like lesions. The arms, hanging loose and straight down, transformed into rubbery tentacles, like octopus' arms. They undulated and swayed as if underwater. The shirt split and fell away as did the pants. The man's flaccid penis also elongated into a wriggling tentacle.

Dave screamed and lurched back. A second scream erupted when more tentacles slithered around the ends of the counter along the floor.

He bolted for the door and almost make it. His hand on the knob, he tripped when one of the squirming appendages encircled his ankle. Grip on the knob lost, he crashed to the floor. He clawed the wood with his fingertips as the tentacle pulled him back toward the counter.

Around the end of the first set of shelves, Dave grasped the bottom of the support. The resistance against the tentacles wrenched his shoulders. With a snap, part of the wooden base tore away. Dave slid across the floor. The monster pull twisted his body, and he ended up on his backside.

He slammed against the end of the counter. For a second, the creature's grip loosened but renewed its hold and its effort to drag him around the counter.

Still holding the spear of shelving support with both hands, Dave torqued sideways, raised his arms, and impaled the tentacle. Viscous green goo spurt like water from a punctured hose.

The slurping noise changed to a high-pitched squeal, like tires skidding on pavement. The tentacle spasmed and released its hold. Dave scrambled to his feet, raced for the door, wrenched it open, and all but dove into his car. He gunned the engine and made a monster-like squeal with the tires speeding out and away from Station 13.

He tried calling the police but discovered his cell phone dead. Maybe the battery had gone bad because he remembered recharging it every night.

Still revved and almost sick with terror growling in his gut, he made it to the abstract office and dropped into the desk chair, labored breaths wheezy.

"What's wrong, Dave?" asked Mary, one of his associates. "You don't sound like you're feeling all right?"

He needed a full minute to regain the ability to speak. "You—won't believe it."

"Won't believe what?"

He opened his mouth to tell his horror story but couldn't find the words. She'd think him crazy. After gathering his thoughts and calming himself, he asked, "Do you ever travel west on Highway 28?"

"Of course," Mary said. "My mother lives in Santa Rio, and I try to visit every weekend."

He nodded. "Have you ever stopped at Station 13?"

"Where?"

"That little gas station a couple miles out of town."

She gave him a patronizing smile. "Dave, I'm sorry, I don't know what you're talking about."

Further description resulted in further confusion and denial any building existed.

"There has to be a record of it," Dave said.

He retrieved a plat map of the county, found the section and coordinates where Station 13 would be located, and dug through drawers to find records. A half-hour later, he sat back, exasperated, and as confused as Mary. No record of Station 13 present or past existed. No name of the place was listed in any directory or area map.

"I don't understand," he said.

Mary shrugged. She'd gone back to her desk and duties.

Another coworker, Bob, had come in a few minutes earlier. "What don't you understand?"

When Dave explained his interest in the gas station—without relating the horrible incident—Bob pursed his lips in contemplation and nodded. "Yeah, it's been a while since I heard about that place."

"So, it exists?" Dave asked.

"Not anymore."

"Bob, I've passed it every day for the last two weeks."

His coworker laughed. "Come on Dave, who you trying to kid?"

"Bob—"

"Listen, my family has been in this town for generations. Why, I don't know, since there's not much to keep us here. Anyway, I said it had been a while since I heard about Station 13. Let me see if can recall the story my grandfather told me."

Bob settled into a chair, tilted back, and placed his feet on top of a desk. "Way back in the 1930s or 40s, there used to be a gas station out west of Sombrio. Small building, a couple pumps, a few bare necessities. Not much, but one of the few places for travelers crossing the desert to fill up."

"If it was named Station 13, there must have been at least twelve others in the area," Dave said.

Bob shrugged. "Don't know about any others. Anyway, what my grandfather told me, seems there was some trouble out there one summer."

"What kind of trouble?"

"Well, he heard this through second and third-hand sources that something weird was reported about the place. You gotta remember, this was a decade or so before the Roswell incident and all the supposed sightings of aliens and UFOs.

"Like I said, he didn't hear too many details 'cept how someone was found dead along the highway near the place. The body was pretty torn up, bloody, and covered in some type of goop. After another victim was found alive long enough to tell the story of his being attacked by some creature, a bunch of townsfolk got together one night, went out, and burned the place. They scattered or buried the remains in the desert, removed the pumps, and buried them, too. Time and Mother Nature have pretty much obliterated any evidence the place existed.

"Why can't I find any records?" Dave asked.

"Ah, Mother Nature again. My predecessor said that in the fifties, Sombrio had a rare cold spell. Temps reached freezing and burst a pipe. Water destroyed a section of storage including all records of Station 13 and a few other county properties. No one had looked at them for years, so the employees at the time could only guess they included the old station. Least none were found."

"And the story your grandfather told was true?"

Bob shrugged. "Who knows? He was a feisty ole coot. Told a lot of stories to us grandkids. Some are probably true; some I knew later were total crap. If the guy who said he was attacked by…something, was telling the truth…if there was even someone, nothing was discussed afterward. The townsfolk let it die. I assumed they buried the victim like they supposedly buried what remained of the station. Nothing more was reported."

The conversation drifted to other topics, and Dave didn't pursue his claim to have driven by, let alone stopped at, Station 13. He clocked out at noon and sped west. Two miles out, he slowed, driving a mere ten miles per hour. After he reached a dip in the road he knew lay beyond the station, he turned around and drove back.

Station 13 was gone.

Another U-turn, he edged the shoulder until a particular cactus that stood next to where the sign had been, showed him where the old station used to be…should have been…had been for two weeks.

He stopped, left the engine idling alongside the road, and exited the car. Nothing existed…wait, not quite nothing. The people who'd burned down the building all those decades ago had sought to remove all signs of Station 13. However, under the sand and scrub grass, Dave discovered chunks of the foundation for the awning over the pumps. Not much, but enough to convince him the place *had* existed.

A thought struck him. If the station hadn't been around since before the middle of the last century…, how had he filled up his gas tank? His gauge still read almost full.

He surveyed a complete circled of the property. An encore of the former terror he experienced not five hours before wormed its way into his stomach, reviving the aching queasiness.

Dust devils twirled by in their endless dance. A wisp of wood smoke drifted into his nostrils. When the breeze died, a faint slurping-sucking sound reached his ears.

He ran for the car and sped away.

From that day forward, whenever Dave came within sight of where Station 13 once stood, he pressed the accelerator to the floor, not slowing until the place was on the horizon in his rearview mirror.

King Valley Marsh Killer
Larry Brown

Deputy Conner zipped his jacket against the evening breeze, shifted his walking stick back into his left hand and with it, pulled aside leaves around the bloody campsite.

He felt it first with the tip, then pulled back the leaves.

"Hey, Sheriff. Found something." He held up a cell phone for his boss to see. On Sundays only Deputy Conner had duty. An evening call from a drone operator about a camp with shredded tent and blood over the surroundings made him call his boss for support.

Puffing, Sheriff Key walked up and took the cell phone from his deputy's hand.

"Well, hope it's the one the hiker had." He fumbled with the phone.

"Oh hell. Here Conner, you turn it on. Maybe the battery's dead anyway."

Conners youthful hands soon had the phone powered up. "What we're looking for Sheriff? Calls? Pictures?"

"Pictures may help. Try those."

After a few thumb tap's, Conner held the phone up. "Look at this video."

The screen was black, but the audio did play a man's voice.

'Something out there. Hey, anyone out there? I'm streaming this to the world. Just so you know.'

The Sheriff looked up at Conner. "Was he streaming? We could get the video that way."

"Nope. It's a bluff. Theres no cell service in King Valley."

A white figure came on screen. It floated up and down, like a man walking, coming towards the phone holder. Tall or short was hard to tell. Its appearance on the black background gave no reference to size. It stopped.

"Looks like he recorded just after dark." The Sheriff commented.

"What is that? A guy in a sheet?" the sheriff asked. "Bet the guy holding the phone is frozen in place. Ha."

They watched another two minutes, until a fog developed in the background. The damp marsh grounds cooling off, formed evening vapor. As the law officers watched, the figure disappeared.

"Oh, crap. Where in the hell did it go?"

"It hasn't moved Sheriff. It's the fog. White on white now."

Movement of the phone brought the campsite into view. A small tent under a tree with a fire beating back the damp air.

On a log an axe and a backpack lay. The man with the camera moved towards the tent.

"Guess he's going for the axe." Conner commented under his breath.

"God, I hope so." The Sheriff wiped his brow.

Jumbled views of the ground, then the tent as the phone flew. It landed, now recording a view of the log where the axe lay. They could see wood tossed on the campfire, increasing its blaze.

"Was he hit or shoved?" The Sheriff asked but knew the answer didn't matter. The man no longer held the phone.

Men's grunts then one of them yelling 'Help.' A thud sound, then silence except for the frogs from the marsh. Their deep croaks muted the sound of something dragged though the dry leaves.

A white clothed figure came into view. The cameras angle recorded its lower half and the log. The flickering firelight outlined the campsite against the intense white background. More of the figure shown as it pulled by the arms, a body, on the other side of the log. Watching the limbs draped over the wood and the axe picked up, made Deputy Conner drop the phone.

"Oh God." His words shuddered the gathering darkness. The Sheriff jumped. Conner picked up the phone.

They watched as the axe came down. With two whacks, the hands detached from the body. Blood spurted across the grounds as the man screamed against the intense pain.

"He's still alive." The Sheriff exclaimed.

The blood stopped squirting.

"He's gone. Like dead." Deputy Conner responded.

The killer jerked at the handless body and brought the head upon the log. Four swings and the head rolled onto the ground. No blood spurted, just a red ooze from the torso.

Conner looked up at the Sheriff, then around them.

"It's getting dark. The mist is coming in. What do we do now.?"

The Sheriff also regarded their crime scene.

"I don't see the body or the killer and it's too dark to shuffle around, searching. Let's get home and bring up the techs and more people tomorrow."

Deputy Conner stood rooted to the ground as a white figure formed behind the sheriff. It gained shape in moments and was taller than his boss. Above his head, it held an axe, with blood-stained handle.

The Sheriff starred at his deputy.

"What's wrong Conner?"

The axe came down, splitting the Sheriff's scull, blood spewing onto Deputy Conner's body cam.

Three months later an FBI agent drove into the crime area. A wildfire soon after the event obliterated all evidence of any crime scene. Firefighters found a body cam attached to a piece of shirt on the side of the road. It left the only evidence available.

The marsh was gone, evaporated by the fire. The brush and trees still lay in their burnt form.

Checking photos taken from the body cam, the agent knew they would never be able to find anything useful.

He wondered if the killer died or would come back after the marsh regenerated and the woods grew again.

A Wendigo of Huron
Paul Benkendorfer

Catherine stood on the balcony overlooking the snow-covered peaks of the Huron Mountains. There was a sense of serenity surrounding them, a calmness that carried with it a tranquility unlike any she had felt before. Having grown up in Phoenix, she had little experience with snow apart from the few trips her family had made up north to Flagstaff or Payson during the winter.

The mountains of Arizona were great, but they were nothing like Huron. Her husband, Keith, had grown up in these mountains with his mother and father, though she had met Keith when they were both studying at the University of Arizona. His mother was from the Ojibwe tribe, although his family lived in Marquette, just off the coast of Lake Superior.

Keith never spoke about her much. All he knew and would tell Catherine was that she died when he was just a boy. According to Keith's father, his wife had gone crazy one night during a blizzard and ran out into the snow. They never found her body. Heartbroken, Keith's father had decided to move to Tucson. She figured he had to get as far away from Northern Michigan as he could. Keith often spoke of a yearning he had to return to the mountains, though a calling of some sort.

She turned around to see her husband standing with two steaming mugs of hot chocolate in his mitten-covered hands. He grinned happily, offering her one. She thanked him and took one. Though the scenery made her happy, she couldn't help but notice that Keith had grown sickly since their arrival. His normal, fiery chocolate eyes had begun to dull to a milky white. His bronze skin and black hair were graying slightly.

The two of them stood together, leaning over the banister, watching the skiers and snowboarders sail down the slopes.

"You okay?" she asked.

"Of course," he said, offering a reassuring grin. He sipped on his hot chocolate and leaned over the banister. "I mean, it does feel weird being back. It all feels so foreign and yet familiar. It's just weird."

"Sure," she said. She leaned over and rested her head on his shoulder. She always felt a sense of comfort around him. And his coat did make quite a cozy pillow. "I told you this would be fun."

"Happy anniversary," he said.

She smiled, clanking her mug against the side of his.

Before he could even take a sip, he began coughing. Much harder than he had before. Keith separated from her and practically buckled his knees with how hard he was coughing. He dropped the mug, causing it to shatter and spill hot chocolate all over the floorboards.

"Keith!" Catherine cried. "Keith, are you alright?"

She placed a comforting hand on his back.

"Yeah," he gagged. "I'm fine."

When he looked up at her she felt a tinge of fear erupt in her chest. His eyes were practically glossed over, the brown fading to an almost encapsulating white.

As soon as they had landed, he had started coughing, but nothing too serious at the time. He had brushed it off as the weather. She accepted the answer but doubted it. She wondered if being back here was bringing about some sort of stress. She had never seen this before.

Cathrine assisted Keith back to his feet.

"Hey, what's that?" a voice shouted.

A flood of murmurs and gasps penetrated through the cold air, but her main concern was for the well-being of her husband. Catherine looked up for a moment to see that just over the peak of the mountains a large, gray cloud was forming and was moving towards the resort at an incredible speed. But that wasn't all that caught her eye. She could have sworn she was something standing atop its peak.

A sudden gust of wind blew by, carrying with it an icy sting that soaked through Catherine's coat and stung her with a cold she had never felt before.

Parents rushed to wrangle their children, while skiers quickly descended the slopes in a mad dash back to the resort. Resort staff shouted for people to remain calm as they ushered guests back inside.

Catherine threw Keith's arm over her shoulder and helped carry him inside. Already, people were rushing to get in. She found a couch in the lobby by the large fireplace located in the center of the room. She laid him down as Keith suddenly began to seizure.

"KEITH!" she exclaimed. She panicked and called for help.

"It's okay," Keith said, weakly. His body settled. "It's okay, Catherine. It's okay–" His words droned off as he collapsed to the floor.

In tears, Catherine grasped his face. To her relief, he was still breathing. She knelt next to him and stroked his hair, waiting for a response.

* * *

"Damn!" Karen snarled, slamming the emergency phone back onto the receiver. Rachael, the new front desk clerk, jumped, frightened. "Sorry," Karen apologized, running a clammy palm through her curly, brunette hair. She hadn't intended to frighten the new hire. Karen was just the same as when she first started. Though never in her twenty years of working in hospitality did she ever experience such a random freak blizzard. Blizzards she had experience with, but never one that came so violently and abruptly without warning. It was like magic.

"Just keep seeing if you can get any kind of signal, okay?"

Rachael nodded meekly. Karen offered her a reassuring smile before strutting off to the lobby. She surveyed the room that was now filled with panicked guests. They had been completely caught off guard by the blizzard. Nothing showed that there should have been any signs of a blizzard on the weather reports.

And neither phones nor internet were working. They had no connection to the outside world. No one to call for an emergency, not that emergency personnel could even make a trip in a blizzard.

Worse yet, one of the guests had fallen ill. A seizure, the wife claimed. The woman, Catherine, had shown Karen her husband. The man was pale and unconscious, but he was breathing. At least that was a good sign. She had some ski patrollers looking into it. They weren't doctors, but at least it put the wife at ease for the time being. Of course, Karen didn't have time to worry too much about that predicament. Some guests complained that others who had been skiing or snowboarding when the blizzard hit hadn't returned yet.

It had been almost two hours. The resort had emergency lights on, and even though a few did manage to trickle in, she didn't have the heart to tell them that if anyone was still lost in the blizzard, they weren't coming back.

She pulled out the walkie-talkie from her hip. "Rich, you there?" she asked.

"I'm here, what do you need, Karen?" a voice on the other side answered.

Rich was the head of maintenance. He was busy in the basement along with Sergio, one of the other maintenance staff, working to make sure there had been no damage to the power grid. The guests were already in an uproar, losing power would only exacerbate the issue.

"How's it looking?"

"Everything is looking fine down here, chief," said Rich. "Nothing wrong. Emergency lines don't seem to be damaged at all."

"What do you think the issue is, then?" she asked.

"No idea," he answered. "Won't know unless we get a good look at the dish outside."

"Can you do it?" she asked.

The dish was only about ten meters off the property. It was dangerous and she didn't want to impose, but if they could get it to work, she could at least try to call someone about the medical emergency they had on hand. They might not be able to get there, but they could at least provide some guidance on how to handle the situation.

"Possibly," he said. "I don't think we'll get much visual out there. I got a flashlight that might help. Can't make any promises, though."

"That's fine. Don't do it if it's too dangerous," she said.

"Shouldn't be," he said. "How's the guest?"

"Don't know," she said. "He looks stable, but the man is going pale really fast. He needs a doctor is all I can say."

"Then we'll go take a look," said Rich. "Don't worry, we won't be out there for too long. If we can't see or do anything, we'll just come right back."

"Are you sure?"

"Positive. Me and Sergio got this."

The radio clicked quiet. Although Karen was thankful Rich would take the risk, she did worry. But both he and Sergio were old veterans of the trade who had been through his fair share of blizzards before. If he was comfortable handling this one, then she wasn't too worried. Rich wasn't the type of guy to take unnecessary risks.

* * *

Catherine fingers combed through Keith's hair as he slept on the couch. He stirred a bit but remained calm. His hair was drenched with sweat and started matting to his face. She didn't know what to do. The personnel had come by and provided what aid they could. They assured her he would be fine, and she hoped they were right.

It had been several hours and people had begun to retire to their rooms for the evening. She looked out the large windows seeing the blanket of white snow gush pass. The light of the day was slowly dwindling to night.

Catherine returned her gaze to her husband, but felt a sudden jolt radiate through her. She had seen something. Something outside that window. She turned her gaze back, not sure if she could make it out, but there were a pair of glossy white bulbs. They almost looked like eyes, but she couldn't quite make out a face or a body. But she couldn't shake the feeling that she was being watched.

Suddenly Keith jerked. She snapped back and held his head, terrified that another seizure was coming on.

"Keith," she said. "Keith?"

Keith's head jerked up, his eyes glossy and white. Almost inhuman.

"Do you hear it?" he asked.

"What?" she asked.

"The voice," he said. "That voice. You don't hear it?"

Catherine looked around the room. The lobby was full of guests murmuring and talking to one another. But she couldn't help but shake the feeling something was watching them. A dark, cold feeling in the pit of her gut.

Her eyes were drawn to a nearby window, where she again thought she saw someone peering in from the outside. It was near impossible to tell in the gusts. It was like a wraith, ghostly with a tall thin body half bent over to get a better glimpse inside. And two balls of cerulean cutting through the snow. Her blood ran cold.

"Catherine?"

She looked down at her sick husband and then immediately backed up. The figure outside slowly stepped away and disappeared into the wind. She prayed it was just her imagination.

"Keith, there are a lot of people talking. Who exactly do you mean?" she asked.

"No, not them," he said, grabbing her elbow. His fingers dug deep into her arm.

"Keith, you're hurting me," Catherine whimpered.

"That voice," he said, frightened. "It's calling me! Oh God, it's calling me!"

They soon drew the attention of other guests. Keith's body began to shiver as he convulsed.

"Keith!"

"What's wrong?" Karen asked, rushing over.

"It's Keith," Catherine answered, tears streaming down her cheeks. "He's saying he's hearing voices."

Keith's body shook and thrashed on the couch, his head snapping around and his body contorting.

Karen pulled Katherine away. Feeling helpless, all Catherine could do was nothing.

Then Keith suddenly lay still. For a moment there was a pause. Everyone watching and waiting. But now it seems to have passed.

"It'll be okay," Karen said, rubbing Catherine's shoulders. "It will be okay."

Karen sat with the disheartened wife, sipping from a mug of coffee one of her staff had brought her and Catherine. Her husband was resting, sleeping restlessly, turning and shaking while sweat drenched his forehead. Catherine diligently wiped it away with the handkerchief Karen had given her earlier.

It was past midnight, and most of the other guests had gone to sleep. Still no luck with the emergency lines, so she would have to hope they could get them to work soon if Keith was going to receive appropriate medical attention. The patrol had informed her not to move her husband and to let him rest. They didn't want him to be disturbed, not in his state. They had tried to administer some painkillers to reduce the fever but none of that seemed to work. Karen knew that the only thing they could really do now was to wait and hope that the blizzard cleared up enough that they could call in an evac.

"Thank you again for the coffee," Catherine murmured. She hadn't taken a sip of her coffee since she got it.

"Of course," Karen replied.

The patrol had already asked what had happened. The poor woman couldn't explain, just that he had collapsed. He had looked and felt a little ill ever since they had arrived in Michigan, but it had not been nearly this bad. Karen didn't know what to say. She had already instructed most of her staff to retire to quarters for the night. Rich and Sergio would venture out in the morning to examine the cables to make sure that there was no significant damage or see if they could somehow reconnect the emergency lines; she had insisted, not wanting them to get lost in the dark.

"So, you're from Phoenix?" Karen asked, a desperate attempt to break the silence.

"Yes," she said. "I grew up there. My husband, he's originally from out here. He's half Ojibwe on his mother's side."

"I see," said Karen, rubbing her chin. "Do his parents still live out this way?"

Catherine shook her head. "No," she said. "His father moved to Phoenix after his mother died. Or after she vanished."

"Vanished?" said Karen. She could see the hurt in the other woman's soft brown eyes. "I'm sorry, I shouldn't pry."

"No, no," said Catherine, offering a forgiving smile, waving it off. "It's quite alright. Keith doesn't talk about his mother too much. I say vanished because…well, they never did find her body. His father said that one night when they were out in the woods camping, his mother just went crazy. He said she was screaming about a voice calling out to her. She snapped and ran out into the blizzard in the middle of the night. No explanation, no reason. She just jumped up in the middle of the night and ran, screaming about a voice."

"That sounds horrifying," said Karen.

"My father-in-law didn't explain more than that," she said. "I insisted, wanting to know about Keith. I could tell, the memory was painful for him, too. He took Keith as far away as he could get. He said something about the mountains, that they're cursed. No," Catherine stopped herself. "He said that his wife said the mountains were cursed. What was it again…the curse of the wendigo?"

"Wendigo?" Karen asked. "I think I've heard a legend about that."

"Really?" Catherine asked, her soft brown eyes filled with intrigue. "What do they say?"

"What do you already know of the wendigo?" Karen asked.

Catherine nodded. "They say they're cannibalistic monsters. The Algonquins said that those who eat the flesh of another human turn into them. And they have those deer antlers."

"Yes, that's the most popular myth," said Karen. "The whole antler thing is a recent phenomenon, it's not really true to the original stories. I've read some stories about wendigos. I'm sort of a fan of that stuff." She smiled.

"My favorite is one about an old Algonquin warrior who was traveling in the woods. He gets word of a monster in those woods who had slain an entire village that resided nearby. Many of his people beg him not to go, but he is a great hero, so he grabs his spear and ventures off. After many days of travel, he comes upon a family deep into the mountains. He finds it rather odd. At first, they welcome him to dine with them and rest for he has had a long journey, but he grows suspicious and tells them he cannot. See, they looked like a normal family, but he could sense something was off about them. Something not human. So, he feigns that he continued on his journey but instead hides in the brush and waits out the night. The next morning, he sees the father with his three sons leave to track him down the path they thought he had set out on. Once they leave, he approaches their camp and discovers that the mother is a wendigo, and bodies of men, women, and children from the tribe are all hanging like cattle on hooks in the tent. The hero kills the mother and goes after the father and sons. Eventually, he finds them, and, after an intense battle, he finally slays the father, but only two of the sons. The third manages to escape the hero and retreats deeper into the forest, never to be seen again. Some say that he still haunts the forest but is still in fear of the warrior. Others say that it is his descendants who now haunt the forest. That their line is cursed, and that they can take human form once they leave, but whenever they return, they revert back to their true form. I don't know why, but it was always one of my favorite local legends."

"That is a strange story," said Catherine.

"It is," said Karen. "There are many legends, but that one always stuck out to me. Like, the idea that wendigos can disguise themselves as humans is just— oooh." She shivered.

Catherine snorted. "Can they also create blizzards?" Catherine asked jokingly.

"Actually," said Karen, "according to the legend, yes, they can."

Catherine sat in solemn silence. Karen could see that her words had bothered the young woman. Keith let out a groan but then went silent.

Catherine reached out, when both she and Karen were startled by the sudden thumping of footsteps thundering down the hall.

"Can't you hear it?!" a man yelled, running out the hallway, dressed only in a plain white shirt and boxer briefs. Karen leapt to her feet, dropping her mug onto the wooden floor. "Can't you hear it?!" the man cried again.

He had gone completely mad. He grabbed at his head like he was trying to pull an invisible entity out of his mind.

"The voice! The voice!" he shouted. Guests began to funnel out of their rooms disturbed by the noise.

"Steve! Steve!" a woman called after him. "What has gotten into you?"

The man ran through the lobby. Karen rushed to go after him but he was too quick. He dashed to the front entrance, all the while yelling about the voice.

"Don't!" Karen shouted as she watched the man throw open the doors.

"Steve!" the woman continued to call after him.

The man laughed maniacally before dashing barefoot outside, disappearing into the blizzard, all the while still yelling about the voices.

Karen reached the front entrance, but she couldn't see. The snow and wind pelted her like icy daggers. She immediately shut the door. She spun around just in time to catch the now sobbing wife.

"Keith!" she sobbed.

The woman collapsed in her arms as Karen held her. Some of the guests had started to gather back into the lobby. She could hear their murmurs of confusion, wondering what had happened. Karen held the sobbing woman and turned to look back through the glass of the front entrance, seeing nothing but snow and darkness.

What the hell had possessed the man to do that? Then she realized the name the woman had been shouting – Steve.

She looked back over at Catherine who was watching. Her soft pink face had gone ghostly pale. *What the hell was going on*?

* * *

The next morning the blizzard was still storming just as hard as it had the previous day. Karen checked the connection and the emergency lines – still down. She was growing frustrated. Already, guests were funneling in for breakfast, and conversing about what had transpired the previous night.

146

Karen roused some of her staff from their slumber to escort the woman back to her room and promised they would send someone to find her husband. A lie, but a comforting lie. The man was as good as dead. They probably wouldn't be able to locate the body until spring, and most likely it would still be on resort premises.

She also had Rich and Sergio help carry the sickly Keith to a nearby room to rest along with his wife.

She sagged in her chair, gripping at her head, exhausted from a lack of sleep. Rachael sat in her chair quietly waiting for instructions on what to do. But what was there to do? The lines were down, and it wasn't like there would be any new guests arriving. Perhaps Karen should send the younger clerk to go check on Catherine and see if she was okay.

"Hey, boss lady," she heard over her walkie-talkie.

She grunted. "Go ahead, Rich," she answered, rubbing her eyes.

"Me and Serg are all set to go check on the cable box. We'll take the maintenance route. Figured it's shorter and easier to trek back if the storm's too harsh."

"All right," she said. "Be careful. We already got one missing. I don't want to file another report."

"Gotcha, no worries," he said. "Won't be out too long. We'll just take a look at the box to see what we can see and head right back in. Save us a cup of coffee, will ya?"

"No problem."

She placed the walkie-talkie on the counter and dropped her head into her hands.

"Keep an eye on the lobby," said Karen. "Let everyone know I'm going in for a nap. Wake me if anything happens."

"Yes, boss," the girl answered confidently.

*　*　*

Catherine sat up-right, taking hold of Keith's hand in hers. Though Karen and the others insisted she get some rest, she just couldn't. She had tried to get some sleep, but she felt as if something was trying to communicate with her. Not that there was a voice, but she could feel as if something was speaking. Calling out to her, to Keith.

"Let him go. Give him to me! GIVE HIM TO ME!"

But why? She shook it off, thinking it was her mind playing tricks on her.

He lay there on the bed, atop the covers. She was worried that by his profuse sweating he still retained a fever, though he was icy cold to the touch. She also began to notice a foul stench emanating from him. She didn't know what it was, but it had to be from the sickness.

Keith stirred a bit.

"Catherine?" he muttered. He turned to look at her, weak and pale. His skin decaying into gray like ash. A white sheen glossing over his eyes. He opened his mouth to speak. It was then she noticed that his teeth appeared to be sharper.

"It's coming – she's coming," he said, swallowing hard.

"Who's coming?" she asked.

"Moth–" Keith began but fell back to sleep.

* * *

Karen was stirred awake by a frantic Rachael. She groaned and rolled over looking at the clock, though her vision was too blurry to read it. Nothing but a bright green in a haze.

"What is it?" she moaned, rubbing her head.

"I'm sorry to wake you, ma'am," said Rachael. "But it's Rich and Sergio."

Karen's vision cleared and she could see the thin, innocent face of Rachael staring at her with bulbous green eyes filled with panic.

"What happened?" Karen asked. "Are they okay?"

"They haven't returned yet, ma'am," said Rachael.

"How long has it been?"

"Two hours."

"Two hours!" Karen shot up alarmed. "Has anyone been able to contact them?"

Rachael shook her head.

"Damn," said Karen. "It was bad enough that some lunatic lost his mind the previous night, but now two of her staff were missing?" She jumped out of bed.

"Let me go get my jacket."

* * *

This storm was colder than any she had endured before. Each flake of snow felt like a shard cutting through her parka down to her bones.

Karen stepped out into the blanket of white. The wind howled with bursts of snow until the world was completely immersed in white. All except the blinking red light where the cable boxes were. She held up her flashlight to help guide her through. Behind her, two other staff members in their own parkas stood by the maintenance door. They insisted they come along with her, but she refused. No, she wouldn't have it. She dared not risk anyone else if she could have it.

She trudged through the snow. Edging her way slowly towards the red light. It was only a good ten meters away from the maintenance door, but it felt like she had trekked a marathon. She passed through the gate and surveyed the area. No sign of Rich or Sergio.

She neared the cable box and she saw the door swaying open in the wind. She noticed something peculiar splattered against the cable box and along the snow beneath it. Her heart stopped.

Blood.

Blood splattered along the cable box, with frozen droplets leading to a pool of red snow.

Then she heard something that made her blood freeze. A screech in the distance. Not like a coyote. It did not sound like any animal she had ever heard of before. The air became putrid to the point she was near suffocating. Every fiber of her being screamed at her to run.

She spun and ran as quickly as her feet could carry her, dropping the flashlight. She stumbled but pressed on. She soon heard the screeching growing louder. The inhuman cry closing in, along with the crunching sound of snow. The stench grew stronger, like that of a rotting animal. Karen fought the urge to vomit.

The maintenance door wasn't far away, but she could see the two staff members she had left behind waving and calling for her to hurry.

She dove towards them, her heart beating in her throat. They caught her and pulled her in.

She turned around, and to her horror she could just make out something standing in the snow. The harsh, snow filled wind veiled the creature to a degree, but she could make out its tall, gangly frame. Twisted, and elongated arms dangled from hunched shoulders of the wraith. Two glowing orbs of cerulean penetrated through the thick haze. The creature hissed and crept back into the storm.

"Bar the fucking doors!" said Karen. "And if we have any guns, get them."

*   *   *

Catherine awoke to find herself in a dark room. She watched his chest rise and fall, indicating that he was at least still alive for the moment. She felt a little relieved, but she could not see anything in the mask of darkness. A putrid stench seemed to hang in the air. It was nauseating.

She turned to a lamp perched on the nightstand beside her and turned it on. When she looked back at Keith she was startled by what she saw. His hair was beginning to fall out and his bronze skin had started to yellow, flecks of skin beginning to fall from his face. His lips seemed to rescind and crack, giving way to what appeared to be a set of fangs.

"Oh my God, Keith," she gasped.

His eyes shot open. They were a soft cerulean beneath a layer of frozen white, like water beneath ice.

"Catherine?" he wheezed. He grabbed at her hand, not able to see. She recoiled at his touch with such a jerk she toppled over the side of the bed, nearly hitting her head on the edge of the nightstand. It was as if she was frost bitten.

"Catherine?" he gasped. "Where are you? Where am I? Do you hear it? The voice. The voice, Catherine. Make it stop. Make it stop, please."

Catherine felt her heart pound in her chest. She peaked over the bed to see Keith had once again fallen asleep.

*　*　*

Karen sat in the basement, still horrified by the image of whatever that thing was out there. Whatever it was, it was what had killed Rich and Sergio. It had tried to kill her.

There was no way this situation could possibly get any worse. Now they were stuck here with some monster roaming outside with no connection to the outside world. She ordered her staff to lock all doors and windows, and not tell the guests anything. The last thing she needed was a massive panic on her hands.

She just prayed that the storm would clear up soon. There weren't any weapons apart from what they could scrounge up. She didn't know what to do, but she was determined to keep everyone safe.

"Ma'am?" she heard Rachael say over the walkie-talkie.

"Yes, Rachael?"

"We have a situation." The young girl sounded frantic.

"What is it?"

"A guest said that she was attacked by something," she said.

Oh, God, Karen thought, dropping her head in her hands.

Guests had gathered in the hallway. Karen weaved and shoved her way through to where she found Rachael, along with two other staff, consoling a hysterical woman. Rachael rushed over to Karen as soon as she spotted her.

"What's going on?" Karen asked.

"The guest said that she was reading in her room when someone broke her window and tried to climb inside."

Karen felt the blood drain from her face. She pushed past Rachael and approached the woman.

151

"What happened?" Karen asked. The woman was still trembling.

"My husband," the woman choked through sobs. "It broke the window. It grabbed and dragged him outside."

Karen sighed. She opened the door and entered the room, met with a rush of cold air. The white, linen curtains whipped and snapped. Shattered glass from the window covered the floor. A trail of blood leading from the bed to the window.

Fuck, she thought. Now the thing was trying to break in

Karen shut the door and turned to the staff. "Keep it locked," she said. "No one goes in. Get her to the medical unit. I don't know what they can do but just get her out of here. Rachael, no one stays in rooms on the first floor anymore."

"Why?" the girl asked.

"Just do it!"

* * *

It had been three days and Keith looked to be in a deteriorating state. By now, his hair had all but withered and fallen from his scalp, and his lips had receded to the point that his teeth, now fangs, were completely exposed. His skin was in decay and his stench grew worse. She wished she could bathe him, but she dared not rouse him from his slumber. Catherine could do nothing but watch from a chair across the bed. She was far too frightened to go near her husband. All she could think was that he was going to die. He hadn't uttered a word in those three days. Food that she had brought from the lounge sat idly on the nightstand, along with an untouched glass of water.

Outside the wind howled and scraped across the glass. It hadn't let up since it started. Catherine prayed – pleaded – that the storm would stop so that Keith could get to a hospital. But it was no use, and now all she could do was watch as her husband withered away on that bed.

So much for their happy anniversary.

She looked at the clock. 7:37 flashed in bright emerald lights on the clock. But she couldn't tell if it was 7:37 in the morning or at night anymore. Could anyone in this storm?

"Catherine?" Keith moaned. Her head snapped up. Her first instinct was to rush over to her husband, but she hesitated. "Catherine? Catherine, you have to let me go. Before it's too late." His voice was raspy, like grating sandpaper.

Keith rolled on his bed and sat up. He was completely bald, and his skin looked like he was a decaying corpse. He turned his head toward her and opened his eyes. She was horrified to see two glowing cerulean lights looking back at her.

She leapt from the chair, her heart beating frantically in her chest.

"Cath–" he his moan crescendoing into an animalistic shrill.

He moved to stand up but toppled over onto the floor. Without a word she ran to the door leading out into the hallway and slammed it shut.

She sagged to the floor, dropped her face into her hands, and began crying.

* * *

The guests were becoming ever more restless and anxious. Karen was beyond exhausted. Guests were in a frenzy. People claimed to hear sounds of scraping on the outside walls and glass being shattered. Others swore they saw a figure moving outside in the snow with reports of blue lights. Every night it was the same. Even on the higher floors. People would alert her to some screaming, she would go to the rooms to find the occupants missing with shattered glass and blood on the floor.

Her staff did what they were told but she knew they were equally terrified. She had to hold it all together, someone had to take charge. Nobody wanted to believe that there was something lurking outside that was hunting guests. But they avoided the windows and doors. Staff even barred any doors leading outside with furniture as best they could.

More and more people grew frantic. Many of the guests even resorted to staying out in the lobby or congregating where there would be a crowd. She often found guests sleeping on or around the couches and furniture. Karen was at a loss. She even heard rumors circulate of people wanting to form a party to go and get help.

Karen tried to reassure them and her staff that everything would be fine. Though she knew they could tell that her words were hollow. Everything was progressively getting worse.

"Folks, I appreciate you and your patience these past few days," Karen said, addressing the crowd. "I understand your frustration, we are all very weary over what is happening."

The worried crowd grew impatient. Some of them jeered at her, demanding to know if help was on the way or there was anything she was doing to keep them safe.

"I am sorry, but until the storm clears up there is nothing we can do," she said.

She could tell that most did not like her answer.

A few people said that they would rather take their chances trying to make it back down the mountain.

"That's guaranteed suicide," she said. "If not, whatever is out there then the blizzard certainly will. Staying indoors is the only sure way we can protect ourselves."

That night she kept watch of the entry door, making sure nobody attempted to leave. Most of her staff had retired for the evening leaving her alone. She had one of the rifles used to ward off bears. If it was good enough for those things, it was good enough for whatever that creature was. Even though much of the panic died down she couldn't be certain someone wouldn't do something stupid.

She caught herself dozing off for a bit. She shook her head, but her blood went cold when she heard the sound of something scraping against the walls outside. Her eyes drawn to the entryway. Nothing but blackness with the swarm of snow. She stood to her feet and listened closely. Whatever it was, it was climbing towards the roof.

She waited to hear what would happen next. Then silence.

* * *

Catherine sat in the hall, outside their room. She could hear creeping on the inside. Then a scratch on the door. She backed away. Then a thud against the door followed by an even louder, more violent thud. Then another and another. There was a momentary pause before another thud came and a slot in the door ripped off.

Catherine stood in horror as two glowing cerulean eyes leered at her, followed by an inhuman shriek that felt like it was going to rupture her ears.

She ran. She ran as fast as her feet would carry her. She didn't know where she was running to, all she knew was that she needed to run as far away from that room as possible.

* * *

Karen stalked through the lobby, keeping her gaze fixated on the roof, armed with the bear rifle. Rachael followed close behind her, the younger girl cowering in fear. Rachael held onto a broom. Useless, Karen knew, but it was at least something.

She prowled around the lobby, holding her hand out to quiet the alarmed guests. They looked about in panic, but she was quick to hush them, jabbing a finger to her lips.

They all listened to the sound of creaking outside as whatever crept slowly by. There was a sudden silence, but it was soon shattered as they heard screaming come from the dining area.

Karen dashed in; Rachael close behind her. She skidded to a stop as she saw the same creature from outside, now kneeling over one of the kitchen staff. The man lay dead in a pool of his own blood as the creature picked up the body with its elongated arms and began to devour the head between its fangs.

Rachael screamed.

The creature snapped its head back around and snarled at them. It dropped the body and lurched towards them, glaring with its glowing cerulean eyes. Karen stepped between the creature and Rachael, holding up her rifle.

"Don't make me whoop your ass," Karen growled.

* * *

155

Catherine reached the lobby where she looked for an exit. The other guests screamed in panic as they ran away. The world around her spun as buddies shoved and pushed by. There was no exit, save for the entrance. Her heart racing and her lungs searing with pain, she spotted Karen and Rachael near the dining area, Rachael turning to run as Karen backed away slowly. A creature, like Keith, creeping towards her.

BANG

The blast echoed through the lobby, followed by a shrill of a shriek as the creature howled.

Through the cries of panic Catherine ran towards her, not knowing where else to go. But as she ran something dropped from the ceiling down impeding her path.

"Keith?"

She looked at her husband – no – he was no longer Keith. He trudged toward her, but another shot rang out, clipping Keith in the shoulder. He howled in pain, dropping to the floor. He looked up at her, his eyes returning to the soft brown she knew.

"Keith!"

"I'm sorry," he croaked.

Screaming, he leapt to his feet, bleeding profusely from his wound, before lunging for the entryway. He shattered through the glass and vanished into the darkness of the storm.

The other creature watched. It leered at Karen who was busy reloading her rifle, careful to keep her eyes steady on the creature. It took a step forward, blood oozing from a wound in its belly. With a final snarl it ran past her and chased after Keith. Then it too vanished into the cold night. Catherine could do nothing but fall to her knees and cry.

* * *

The next morning the blizzard finally cleared, and the phone lines were working again. Karen picked up the phone to call for emergency rescue, then hung up. There was a sense of relief that swarmed through the resort. For now, the nightmare was over. It was finally over.

Emergency services had been called, and now all they could do was wait. Karen slouched in her chair resting her head on the barrel of the rifle. The phone rang and Rachael answered.

"Excuse me, Ms. Potter," Rachael said, holding the phone. "It's Mr. Gilbert. He wants a detailed report of what happened."

Karen took the phone. "Hello, Mr. Gilbert?" she said. "Yeah, before you say anything, sir, I just want to let you know…I quit."

With that she hung up the phone and sat back down. She flashed Rachael a proud smile who returned it with one of her own.

* * *

It was another week before Catherine would be able to return home to Phoenix. She had to explain to the police what had happened to her husband. There was no way they would ever believe that he had turned into some sort of monster and disappeared into the blizzard. Nobody really could tell what had actually happened. She just said that she didn't know. That he had gone mad in his illness and ran outside.

After a year she still carried her wedding ring, wondering what had ever happened to Keith. She never dared return to the Huron Mountains. In her mind, he was long gone. But she missed him.

On the night of their next anniversary, she heard a knock on her apartment door.

She got up to answer it, but she didn't want to be disturbed. This was her night of remembrance.

"Catherine?" She heard a familiar voice say: It was Keith. "Catherine, open up, sweetheart. It's me!" The knocking continued.

The Haunting of Four Mile Creek
Deb Miller

Straining to see through the warm, misty night, Gail Campbell pedaled carefully along a twisted asphalt bike trail. The black path snaked alongside Four Mile Creek as it meandered through a suburban, densely wooded greenway. A dim light beam from her helmet reflected rather than pierced the late August drizzle.

With envy, she imagined everyone in their dry homes and burrows sleeping peacefully like the dead. Everyone except for that predator ahead, who was peeking at her from the undergrowth. The instant her faint helmet light revealed two glowing eyes in the blackness, they vanished.

Actually, she couldn't tell by its eyes if it was a predator. Once again, she'd jumped to a conclusion. Maybe the critter was some creature's frightened prey. In any case, tonight was not peaceful. Tonight was dangerous.

She regretted not buying batteries for her headlamp. She could have. She had intended to. The convenience store carried them. If tonight's fog thickened, it would become too treacherous to keep riding. She'd be forced to walk her bike home.

Her tires hissed as they rolled through the thin layer of rainwater coating the path. She felt them spray painting a stripe up the back of her store uniform. In a bike bag fastened under her seat, she'd stuffed in a bicycle shirt earlier in the day, just in case she needed it. She could have changed into it before leaving the store. She knew the forecast threatened rain. That was why she'd brought it.

In her experience, things normally worked out for the best. An optimistic nature was something she was proud of. This time, however, her sunny attitude had likely ended in a stain ruining her uniform. Her mother's voice criticized her thoughts. "Gail, why do you always jump to conclusions?" She didn't. She'd prepared ahead. A boss once advised her to make a "Plan B" so if she misjudged a situation, she'd have a course of action. Well, Plan B doesn't help if you still misjudge a fickle situation. Another regret to add to tonight's grim tally.

To each side of her elm, cottonwood, sycamore, and oak worried her as their bone breaking trunks crowded the trail in this section. Their branches of wet leaves whispered like spectators watching a funeral procession.

About forty feet up the trail, a ghostly six-foot-high pile of mortared river rock materialized from the fog. She'd been watching for it. This historical marker meant the trail's parking lot waited a mere quarter mile further on. From there, streetlights would illuminate the remaining mile of what at this hour would be an empty four-lane roadway to her apartment.

Chest and jaw muscles relaxed. That surprised her. She hadn't realized how tense she'd gotten. She shifted into a faster gear upon passing the marker.

It always saddened her to think of the disaster the marker commemorated. One hundred and forty-six years ago, twenty people were killed and 35 injured as a result of the August 29, 1877, Four Mile Creek train wreck.

It was raining on that tragic night too. The marker said the creek became a torrent and undermined the railroad bridge. When the steam engine raced onto it at 2:30 a.m., the bridge collapsed.

With that thought, three events occurred to Gail simultaneously. To her left, she heard a massive steam locomotive explode and several train cars tumble into the creek. Her bike flashed through a six-foot shimmering cloud on the trail. And an Arctic stab of cold jolted her.

Her hands choked the handlebar brake levers. Both bike wheels locked and the rear tire fishtailed to the right. Skidding out of control, she careened off the trail; side swiped the bark of a tree trunk; and cannon balled over her handlebars into a thicket.

She remained still, waiting for the pain. This wasn't her first bike crash. The pain would come, and it would inform her of her injuries. Soon she could tell that a broken branch poked her lower back. How deeply was she impaled? Stinging flared along her left arm below the short sleeve of her work uniform. Her left leg also smarted. After another thirty seconds, she decided the bush branch had only punched rather than stabbed her. She was very lucky as bicycle accidents go. Struggling to extricate herself, she sank deeper into tangled branches and a mass of wet leaves.

"Ma'am, may I assist you?" It was a man's deep, raspy voice - a smoker's voice?

She froze. No one was supposed to be out here. Her helmet light illuminated the green cocoon of her trap. It probably revealed her location, so she turned it off. She hadn't seen the man, so she could only assess the threat he posed by his voice. The deep, raspy tone made her picture a large, rough man. Would he hurt her?

From the time she started school as a child until she left home, her mother warned her about men. "They'll grab you and cover your mouth," her mother would say. "They'll hurt you. No one will hear your screams." As she grew older, she'd understood the sexual nature of the hurt her mother meant: humiliation, torture, rape, and death. But those horrors weren't the end of the abomination.

Her imagination pictured her naked, bloated body in a soybean field. It would be a stinking, rotting corpse, partially eaten by predators. The nightmare always included crows aggressively fluttered and cawing threats at each other as they pecked out her eye sockets. A half a dozen rats crawled over her torso, chewing on her intestines. Coyotes snarled and snapped other pack members away as their jaws ripped off a chunk of thigh muscle.

What if this guy's polite offer to help actually came from her long-anticipated childhood monster? Her ankle tingled. Any second, his powerful hand would grasp it and yank her to him. She had to escape. Quietly, she rolled right, then left. The bush held her firmly in its embrace. Why hadn't he latched onto her? Was it possible he couldn't find her? It was very dark, and the rain was drowning out sound. Perhaps she'd could remain very still until he left. What if he didn't leave? His lust for her might be powerful.

What if she was jumping to conclusions again? What if he was a decent man? If he thought she was injured, would he abandon her? He'd want to help her. He might call 911. In either case, the best action to take might be to stay hidden. Whether a rescue team or a bicyclist came, if she heard voices, she could call out for help then.

Being as dark as a tomb, her only source of information was the pattering of a light rainfall on the leaves of her bush prison. Was he searching for her? If he was, she couldn't hear it. Was he standing still, listening for her to make a sound?

An Arctic jolt of cold froze her into a solid ice sculpture. She couldn't move or breathe. She couldn't even blink. Then, like a magician's trick, she rose out of the thicket, out to the path, and was laid on the wet trail. Released from her caught-in-the-bush statue pose, she collapsed like a rag doll onto the asphalt. She made a final violent shiver. Staying low, she rolled over and got her feet under her. Where was he?

"Name's Edgar." His voice had an odd, buzzy modulation to it. Which direction had it come from? The night was still as dark as a grave. She had to escape, but any direction she chose could lead straight to him.

"You from the train?"

She thought, what train?

Anguished screams, desperate cries for loved ones, and hissing steam assaulted her. The decibel level was incredible. It was inescapable even as she pressed her palms to her ears. She screamed repeatedly as the sounds of the disaster went on and on.

A clap of thunder replaced the horrible sounds of despair with silence. In the blissful quiet, she heard only her own gasping. Relieved, she knew the auditory ordeal was over. Now if she could just get her breath back.

Her relief died with a new thought. Had the fellow read her mind? That was ridiculous. Then again, she hadn't spoken a word, but only thought about her question. No! She wouldn't consider such nonsense.

His magic trick of lifting her out of the thicket meant he knew exactly where she had hidden. While he might not need light to find her, she needed it to find him.

Switching her helmet light back on, the woodland glistened. As she pivoted around, the surrounding vegetation danced with sparkles, but her panning revealed no one. He must be behind a tree or bush.

She answered his question. "No, I'm not from the train." Then a thought occurred to her. "But you are, aren't you?"

Edgar's reply came from a specific direction this time: from the creek. He ignored her question, and as he spoke, his voice faded in and out of static. "I … horse … get to … must stop her."

This guy was nuts. She opened her mouth to speak and then wondered if any uncooperative comment would trigger an even worse punishment than a brain numbing sound. This night might end better if she pretended to assist him.

"I might be able to help you. Who is it you need to stop? Maybe I can take you to her."

The voice was buzzier and came from her left. She understood most of it.

"Her fam… is force…. to wed … cad, Alfred, this … day."

That some supernatural stuff might be going on was just too weird an idea to accept. Yet how else could she explain the crazy train wreck noise? That had been painfully real. If it were a hoax, he could have set up a professional rock band sound system. Not likely out here. That could explain it, but an electric source was about a quarter of a mile away.

What about her levitation? Nothing could do that. Not in the real world. She did not believe in them, but a demon could. She'd seen the Exorcist. Lots of religions believed in demons. The occult did too. The Bible had prophets casting out demons. Demons were always portrayed as evil tormentors.

If this guy was supernatural, she hoped he was a ghost. She didn't believe in them either. But she figured if they did exist, they were ordinary people who happened to be dead. There were evil people. Like serial killers. Was her ghost an insane psychopath? What if he levitated her 200 feet into the air and dropped her? He could be dangerous.

She turned her thoughts back to his last statement. How should she interpret his reference to "this very day"? Was it the same day as the historic train wreck? She had to be very careful with her next moves. "I need to get to my bicycle."

"No, you need … help me find … horse." The modulation was cleaner and louder.

"To do that, I need to get my phone from my bike bag."

"I … no idea … talking about." Varying degrees of static overpowered the angry voice coming from the woods behind her and to her right. She looked, but no one was there.

"My bike is metal with two wheels. A phone is … sort of a telegraph machine." How could she explain about Google search?

From the darkness, she heard bush and leaf movement. Her bike rolled upright into her helmet light. She grabbed a handlebar and claimed her phone from the bag.

"The girl you need to stop. What's her name? Do you know where she lives?"

She jumped when the voice spoke a foot in front of her. No one stood before her in her helmet light.

"Alice Catell."

Concentrating on her search app, her tension eased a bit. None of the results were the woman's name. Listed results showed only as alternate possibilities weren't even in the state, let alone Des Moines. At least they weren't going to terrorize a living woman tonight.

"She lives near Hoyt Sherman's house." There was still static in his voice, but she heard each word clearly.

"I know where that's at. Do you want me to take you there?"

His voice came from forty feet away towards the creek. It was unintelligible static.

"I can't understand you. Can you say it again?"

Inches from her face, a clear voice bellowed. "I can't leave!" Then, in a normal volume, he said, "I've been trying to go to Alice, but I can't leave the wreck. I go in a straight line in any direction and end up back at the wreck."

"Are you going to hurt me if I leave you?"

"What? Of course not."

"If I go, I will find Alice. I will tell her you are here, waiting for her." After thirty seconds of silence, she asked, "May I go?"

A shimmering oval of dim light took ten seconds to grow from a small spot to six feet. Finally, like a snowy actor walking up to a snowy TV channel camera, she made out a human shape. From the static man, a raspy voice said, "You won't come back. They never do."

The oval faded.

"I will. I promise." Why had she said that? She was never ever coming back here. "Can you tell me her father's name or give me her address?"

She waited for the ghost to speak again. Except for branches rustling in a warm breeze, it was quiet. The rain had stopped, and the fog was wispy thin. He could still be lurking, watching. Despite his denial, he still might hurt her. He still might be her dreaded childhood monster. Carefully, watching for his sudden reappearance, she pedaled slowly along the trail to the road. Relieved to be out of the woods, she pushed hard for home.

* * *

In the weeks that followed, Gail researched the name Alice Catell. The only Catells in Des Moines in 1877 were Mr. John Catell and his wife Doris. He was the 1st violin of the Des Moines orchestra, and she was at one time the vice president of the Women's Suffrage and Union Relief Society. Gail made no headway with Alice's fiancée. A lot of men named Alfred lived in the city. If she couldn't figure out Alice's married last name, she was at a dead end.

As weeks turned into months, then into a year, she thought of her ghost only occasionally. At night, if a train whistle blew or if traffic stopped for a crossing train, she would feel guilty. His last words to her were prophetic. She was like all the other, who never returned.

Her ghost haunted her conscience. Not literally, but her guilt did. She'd promised him she'd find Alice and return and she hadn't. Gail knew she wasn't ever going to find a living Alice to bring to him. But she wanted to find out what had become of her. Did Alice have children? Did she and Alfred have a happy life together? How long had she lived? Where was she buried? She wanted to tell Edgar all these things. Perhaps then he could find peace. She hoped telling him and having him realize they were both dead wouldn't make matters worse.

Frustrated, she knew there was no need for her to worry about it. It was unlikely she'd ever find anything, and his current suffering would go on forever.

On July 4th, that situation changed. At a family picnic, her cousin talked about his genealogical research. Emboldened, she told him about her own research obstacle with a historical romance novel she was writing about Edgar and Alice. Could he help her?

There were, he said, ways to get around such roadblocks. He shared a couple of his miraculous research successes. Gail hired her cousin and set him to searching for Alice.

That's why this August 27th, at 1:30 a.m. she stood by her car under a starry sky in the Four Mile Creek bike trail parking lot. In her backpack was the book her cousin had written and printed on the life of Alice Catell Keplin. Would it matter that the weather was clear? She hoped her ghost, Edgar, would show up tonight. If not, she'd come next year, and the year after that. She'd come until she was too old and frail to come anymore.

Giving her surroundings a sudden, quick survey, she glimpsed movement. Across the street from the greenway park, was an apartment complex. She stared at a second-floor window. The curtains were open. The room was dark. To be sure, she focused her attention there, where she thought the movement had come from. Nothing. She was imagining things.

Down the street and out of sight, she heard a vehicle approaching. It was time to go. Hurrying into the bike trail entrance, she stopped and watched as a pickup truck drove past. Its headlights disappeared over the crest of a hill. Good. No predators would follow her on her isolated quest.

It took her only a few minutes to jog the quarter mile to the train wreck marker. Her husband, Kyle, had wanted to come with her. He knew of her fear of isolated places. He didn't have to remind her, but he did. It was dangerous, he'd said, for a woman to be alone in a park at night. Eventually, they compromised. She came alone, but Kyle insisted she call him every few minutes with a status update.

At the wreck monument, she clicked off her flashlight and waited in the dark. She thought of the book in her backpack. Her ghost would be disappointed. Alice had married Alfred Keplin as planned. They had six children and a long life together, building a haberdashery on Court Avenue. Her genealogist cousin had found historic pictures of their business, houses, schools, children, grandchildren and finally, her grave. The final page of the book was a picture of her headstone in Woodland Cemetery. Gail's cousin, bless his heart, had cleaned it and put down a vase of flowers before taking its picture.

Looking at her phone, it was 2:29 a.m. Almost time. After a minute, she walked south on the trail to where she thought her ghost had appeared. Tonight it was not raining, but it was warm and humid like a typical Iowa August night.

"You came back!" The raspy voice, which had terrified her so, spoke with the same odd, buzzy modulation she remembered.

"Yes, Edgar, I did. And as promised, I found her." Gail held out the journal. A small spot of light grew into a large oval coming from the direction of the creek. "Can you see her picture?"

"Yes," said a soft, clear voice. "That is Alice. Why isn't she with you?"

Gail turned to the last page of the book and held it out toward the oval light. "I'm sorry Edgar. She died over 90 years ago in 1932 at the age of 73."

The oval light blinked out. "Edgar? Edgar, I have more to tell you."

Footsteps walked quickly up the asphalt trail from the direction of her car. "Kyle, I said I would call you."

The dark shape that approached was not her husband. "Don't you know not to walk into a dark place at night? No one's going to hear you scream, Sugar. Not out here. Hey, now, don't you try to run from me."

He grabbed the back of her head as she turned to run. Giving her shoulder length hair a yank towards him, he pulled her off balance and onto her rear end. He laughed. "We're going to have some fun, you and I."

She didn't want to cry. She needed to see to fight, but tears flowed, blurring her vision. He was her childhood monster! It wasn't her imagination early tonight that saw movement in the apartment window. He'd been there, watching - and lusting for her. And now? Now he had her. Now he was going to humiliate her. And now she was going to die.

Sitting on her hips, he squeezed her chest while she gasped in pain. He laughed again. A halo of light behind his head hid his face in shadow. She was glad for the shadow. She didn't want to see his expression.

The halo grew larger and brighter. Then shrieking and crashing of an oncoming train wreck consumed all of her senses with its enormity. It went on for thirty seconds, maybe. Would it deafen her this time? It was louder than the first time, wasn't it? Then, as if from a switch, silence.

She lay on the bike trail, panting.

"Are you hurt?"

Lying on her back, she twisted her head about to locate Edgar. "Not seriously. Where's … you know."

"He's with me. Well, actually, he's experiencing the train crash in a permanent and very personal way. No, don't ask me anymore questions about him."

Gail stood to her feet. "Edgar, I can see you. Sort of. You're pretty blurry, but I think you held up your hand to stop my question."

"Good. I hoped my force was enough. I won't be able to maintain it for long." Looking at Alice's book lying on the ground beside the trail, he said, "Tell me everything about my beloved's life."

So Gail retrieved the book and turned the pages for him. She read each page and explained each family tree chart down to Alice's living dependents. On the last page, she once again showed him the picture of her grave.

"She had an average life, but a happy one. Her only fame was with her hat customers, family, and friends who loved her."

Edgar's image flickered. "Thank you for this."

"Edgar, I think she might like you to visit her. Do you know how to go to her?"

"It never occurred to me that either of us was dead. I don't know if I can. I'm thunderstruck."

"Are you still a captive of the train wreck? Now that you know the truth, has your situation changed?"

After a moment, he smiled. "Yes, it has. I think I can leave." He paused for another moment. "I'm sure of it. I can go to her." He bowed to Gail and disappeared.

After putting Alice's genealogy into her backpack, she called Kyle. "Hi, Honey. It worked. Edgar moved on."

"I'm so happy for you … and for Edgar. Are you coming straight home?"

"Yes, I'm exhausted. I'll be there in a few minutes. Love ya."

Jogging to her car, she was on high alert. True, Edgar had eliminated a monster from the Earth tonight, but fate had not assigned this guy to her at birth. There were millions of predators stalking and killing women all over the world. That frightened her far more than a ghost.

Crescent City
Anthony Samuels

From the capital city of Richmond, where I completed medical school, I moved into a large, one-bedroom apartment on Canal Street in New Orleans, not far from the cemeteries. Since the city was built below sea level everyone was buried above ground in crypts and mausoleums. The "Crescent City", as it was called, was kept dry by complicated systems of levees and canals constructed throughout the years by the Army Corps of Engineers. A bend in the Mississippi River was the basis for the analogy with a crescent moon.

I rented the best place I could find on my intern's salary. It was the upper half of a two-story building. The bottom half was shared by a chiropractor's office and a small burrito factory. I split the upper half with an older single woman. We each had a one bedroom, one bath apartment, identical except for our views. Hers was of several large elm trees and other two-story homes. My view was of the windowless solid brick wall of a two-story business next door with a doughnut shop on the corner that never closed.

I thought we were going to get cancer from the radiation produced by the x-ray equipment downstairs, in spite of the chiropractor's assurance of lead shielding. The constant aromas from the Mexican food and the doughnuts wafting up from below sent our olfactory bulbs into a frenzy. Not to mention the roaches or "palmetto bugs" as they were called. They were so large one could actually hear them tiptoeing under my bed in the middle of the night. Till then I didn't know that roaches could actually fly. Across the street in this residential area far from downtown, was an old movie theater that began showing artsy movies when their business started to falter. A rock through their front window from a disgruntled patron put an end to that practice.

My next-door neighbor was the most bizarre lady. She was of average height and build with shoulder length jet black hair which distinctly contrasted with her milk white skin, large red lips, and heavy eye shadow. Her hazel eyes sparkled iridescently with rich hues of brown and green. She always wore the same style matronly dress that was below the knee in length and as black in color as pitch. The woman reminded me of "Morticia" from The Addams Family without the frivolities.

To add to her mystique, she was very reclusive and was rarely seen outside of her apartment. I never heard a sound through the wall that we shared. No voices, radio, television, or even a vacuum cleaner. She never had any guests. When we happen to pass each other in the hallway, she never made eye contact with me or even said "hello." To say our stairwell was poorly lit would be more than generous. The solitary ceiling lightbulb was too difficult to change whenever it surpassed its lifespan. The rooms were all so tall, one needed an extension ladder just to change the expended bulb. One night returning home late from grocery shopping after work, I struggled to walk up the stairwell with a bag full of foodstuffs. I could not even visualize the steps or handrail, feeling around in the dark by shuffling my feet forward and with my free hand in front of me.

It was so dark about midway from the top I had to stop to get my bearings and reorient myself. Then, for some unknown reason, my instincts told me to look to my left. Through a veil of darkness, I could barely discern the outline of a cloaked figure standing next to me, sharing the same step.

"Ahhhhh!" Having the life frightened out of me, I screamed so loud I thought the police would be summoned. It was my neighbor with her back pressed firmly against the wall to avoid any physical contact with me. Dressed perennially in black, she never made a sound or said a word. Then she ran upstairs to return to her apartment like a banshee.

Meanwhile my startle reflex caused me to throw my arms up into the air along with my bag of groceries. Cans of Campbell's pork and beans, Del Monte pineapple, and condensed milk along with some fresh vegetables and apples went cascading down the stairs with an ear shattering sound.

I never saw my mysterious neighbor after that episode until one day when there was a loud, forceful knock on my apartment door. Much to my surprise were four very large men dressed in dark business suits with bulges under their jackets. The badges they produced had the letters "ATF" embossed on them.

"Hello. Dr Branch? I am Agent Carrera – Alcohol, Tobacco, and Firearms. These gentlemen behind me are my associates. Do you know a Mrs. Gladys Thibodaux?"

"Yes. My next door neighbor. I don't even know her first name - just the last name of Thibodaux on the mailboxes downstairs," I replied.

"We need to talk to her. Can you show us to her apartment door?"

I lead the entire entourage down the long, darkened hallway to her apartment's unmarked doorway.

We did not get a response when we knocked several times. After jimmying open the door, we found my neighbor without her signature black dress on, kneeling completely unappareled on the living room floor. She was curled in a fetal position, trembling uncontrollably. Her ill kept apartment had food and garbage strewn on the floor with numerous papers and documents scattered about the furniture. The scene was reminiscent of the aftermath on Bourbon Street of another Mardi Gras. Eventually she was whisked away by the agents in a dark, unmarked sedan resembling those in the sixties TV series Dragnet.

The next day I ran into the chiropractor, who owned the entire building. He told me the lady worked at the ATF office downtown and didn't show up for work for two weeks. She apparently suffered from mental health issues and went off her meds. Because of her sensitive position at the agency, they came looking for her after not answering her telephone. From the appearance of her apartment and her mannerism, I would have never guessed she worked at the ATF in such a lofty position.

Our chance encounter on the stairwell that night left an enduring, haunting impression upon me. I have personally not known anyone, like my neighbor, who I just witnessed have such a departure from reality as this woman. It had engendered in me a greater sense of empathy towards those grappling with mental illnesses. My upcoming rotation in psychiatry begins in December, an unstable time of the year for the mentally challenged. I shall be looking forward to it.